Had it
she'd a

Was it just this afternoon that Keeley had walked away from that wedding chapel, leaving behind Troy and her dreams of a future with him? Had it been only an hour ago that she'd been limping back to the hotel, nestled against a sexy stranger? A stranger named Digby...

Suddenly she heard a sound from the room next to hers. A shuffle of sorts. Digby, tossing in his sleep? Or Digby, not sleeping, as he'd predicted.

The way I'm not sleeping. Alone. Lonely. Frustrated.

She sat up. There were plenty of reasons why she should stay where she was, but she didn't want to think of them now. She didn't want to think at all. She only wanted to bury her face in Digby's broad chest and have his strong arms around her.

And not five feet away from her, there was a man who'd made it clear he wanted the same thing.

Keeley got out of bed. Holding her breath, she pulled the connecting door open, ready to knock on the door to his room. But it was already open. Taking two steps forward, Keeley whispered his name. And suddenly she wasn't alone anymore....

Despite her glamorous career as a romance novelist, **Glenda Sanders** has a passion for rummaging through thrift and antique/junk stores in search of comical pigs and cows, and she loves letting her characters loose in the dusty, hole-in-the-wall places she loves. "Any man who not only tolerates such shopping trips but understands them is truly a hero," she says. "Now, *there's* a fantasy!" Her own personal hero, Russell, is just glad that the total at the cash register on her shopping marathons is usually under ten bucks!

Books by Glenda Sanders

Don't miss any of our special offers. Write to us at the following address for information on our newest releases.

Harlequin Reader Service
U.S.: 3010 Walden Ave., P.O. Box 1325, Buffalo, NY 14269
Canadian: P.O. Box 609, Fort Erie, Ont. L2A 5X3

Glenda Sanders
NOT THIS GAL!

Harlequin Books

TORONTO • NEW YORK • LONDON
AMSTERDAM • PARIS • SYDNEY • HAMBURG
STOCKHOLM • ATHENS • TOKYO • MILAN
MADRID • WARSAW • BUDAPEST • AUCKLAND

To my editor Brenda Chin,
who deserves a halo for her patience.
Thanks for hanging in there.

ISBN 0-373-25741-4

NOT THIS GAL!

Copyright © 1997 by Glenda Sanders Kachelmeier.

This edition published by arrangement with Harlequin Books S.A.

® and TM are trademarks of the publisher. Trademarks indicated with
® are registered in the United States Patent and Trademark Office, the
Canadian Trade Marks Office and in other countries.

Printed in U.S.A.

1

"DEARLY BELOVED, we are gathered here, in the presence of—"

The tackiest plastic flowers on the face of the earth, Keeley Owens thought, attributing her knit-picking pettiness to bridal jitters. She should be concentrating on the ceremony, but the setting was too surreal. The endless loop of "Going to the Chapel" filtered through the walls to provide an ambience of crass commercialism. She'd always dreamed of a dusk wedding in a country chapel with no lighting except for candles, not a midafternoon ceremony in a Las Vegas chapel with plastic Victorian gingerbread trim.

"...to join together this man—"

Keeley looked at the groom's face, a face that set female hearts aflutter, and tried to concentrate on the significance of the moment. She was standing beside Troy Mitchell, exchanging marriage vows. Did it matter where they were?

She peered into his midnight blue eyes. Bedroom eyes. Eyes that could seduce from across a room and twinkle with boyish mischief as he mentally undressed a woman he'd never even met. Today those eyes were glassy and his beautiful features were rigidly set.

"...in Holy Matrimony."

Troy's Adam's apple bobbed above the bow tie of his rented tuxedo. He'd had a lot to drink, but not enough to make him totally oblivious to the depth of the commitment implied in the word *matrimony*. He'd always referred to marriage as Unholy Acrimony and for the first time, Keeley wondered where he'd heard it. It was far too clever a play on words for Troy to have come up with it on his own. Troy was a doer, not a thinker.

"Do you—" The officiating justice of the peace frantically searched through the papers atop his book of ceremonies for the name he needed before continuing, "Kelly Owens—"

"Keeley," Keeley corrected reflexively. Her cheeks burned with embarrassment. Everyone was staring at her as though her adamant correction had been a breach of etiquette. "It's Keeley, not Kelly," she said firmly.

She was only going to do this once, and she'd be damned if she was going to let him get away with saying her name incorrectly.

"Do you *Keeley*, take this man—" He referred to the papers again. "*Troy Mitchell*, to be your lawfully wedded husband?"

Keeley opened her mouth, but the words refused to come.

The notary cleared his throat. "The traditional responses are 'I will,' or 'I do.'"

Keeley sensed the air of expectancy as everyone waited for her to speak, but the words stuck in her throat. Apparently the official was accustomed to nervous brides, because he chuckled amiably. "Perhaps we should start over. Do you, Keeley, take this man, Troy—"

She looked again at Troy's beautiful face. Grinning cockily, he swayed unsteadily. He'd had a *lot* to drink.

"No!" she said emphatically, surprising even herself with her vehemence. "No. I don't. I can't. I...won't—"

Troy cursed violently. "What in the hell is wrong with you? You've been nagging me to marry you for over a year."

Keeley pressed her fingertips to his archangel face. "You don't want to marry me, Troy."

He cursed again. "Hell, Keeley, I'm here. What more do you want?"

"I want a man who doesn't have to get drunk in order to make himself marry me."

"I'm not drunk," he said. "I've just been celebrating a little."

"Men don't marry women because they win five thousand dollars at a slot machine. Men marry women because they love them and want to build a life with them."

"Come on, Keeley. We've been living together for months. We might as well be married."

He said it with the same resignation with which he would have said, "We might as well be dead," and she knew that's exactly how he felt about marriage—if he'd been sober enough to actually feel anything.

"You know you're my woman," he said, automatically turning on the charm that so often worked for him.

"No, Troy. I'm not your woman. I'm your main squeeze." He'd called her that often enough. "You're not a man, Troy. You're an overgrown boy, and you always will be." A tear slid down her own cheek as she mourned the dreams she'd once had about their future together. She'd been a starry-eyed college student fresh from the country when she'd met him. And Troy, virile, beautiful and naturally charming, had seemed like the God of Big-City Cool. She'd been flattered when he'd noticed her and bowled over when he'd singled her out. They'd become lovers and, eventually, she'd moved into his apartment—complete with dreams of marriage, home and family.

She lifted her fingertips to his cheek. "I'll always love you, Troy. I'll always treasure the time we spent together. But we took it as far as it would go, and it would be a mistake to try to take it any further."

Troy's expression turned ugly. Vile. "You little—" Shoving her away with drunken clumsiness, he called her a list of names, each more demeaning than the one before.

While she knew it was the booze talking, the horrible names were like spikes piercing Keeley's heart. She flung her bouquet to the floor at Troy's feet. "Thanks for making it easier!"

Spinning, she tore from the hideous faux-Victorian chapel with its plastic flowers, bad sound system and cheap electric candles. She could have been fleeing a dungeon after years of confinement for the sensation of freedom that swept over her as she stepped into the sunshine and dry desert air.

She paused on the gingerbread-balustraded porch to get her bearings. What was she supposed to do now? She was miles from the hotel, the sandy shoulder of the divided highway that ran in front of the chapel looked far from welcoming and her spike heels were hardly conducive to walking.

A backward glance through the window showed

Troy being coddled and comforted by his friends. *His* friends. They'd always socialized with *his* crowd, never with hers, and this crazy trip to Vegas was no exception. Their traveling companions, the would-have-been witnesses to their wedding, were his friends, her acquaintances. As unappealing as the prospect of walking through sand in spike heels might be, it beat riding back to the hotel with four people who would undoubtedly regard her as the coldhearted witch who'd just jilted Troy Mitchell. She'd be about as welcome with that bunch as an armadillo on a golf course.

She walked to the road, looked down the long expanse of sandy shoulder and lifted her chin in resolve. If she set out now, she might make the hotel before dark. Drawing in a deep breath, she took the first step of what she knew would be a long trek.

The sand was even more difficult to walk in than she'd anticipated. She tried walking on the balls of her feet, but the heels were too high for her to hold the sharply tapered tips above the surface. And although it appeared to be solidly packed, the surface sand yielded to the stiletto points like soft butter, swallowing them each time she put her foot down. Why, oh why, had she let Troy talk her into the ridiculous shoes anyway?

Because he'd thought they were sexy. Just as he'd thought the thigh-high lace stockings and fingerless gloves were sexy. Just as he'd thought the absurd dress with the stretch-lace bodice with its plunging V back and full, layered lace miniskirt with handkerchief-tip hemline and row after row of narrow lace trim was sexy. Hitting a jackpot had put him in a wild and crazy mood and, as usual, she'd tried to be as wild and crazy as he was.

So what else was new? She'd been trying to keep up with Troy's wildness for almost three years, constantly trying to prove herself to be as unconcerned for conventionality as he was. She could see now that she wasn't cut out to be "wild and crazy" the way Troy was. She'd outgrown the need to be uninhibited and devil-may-care—just as Troy would never outgrow it. They were fundamentally different, fundamentally unsuited to each other. She wanted a pet, he wanted an annual pass to the pubs, bars and saloons of Church Street Station; she wanted to plan for a house and a child, he wanted to plan for a lakeside condo and a jet ski. She'd been trying too hard to hold on to the idea of being Troy Mitchell's woman to accept the truth.

By the time she'd gone a few blocks up the road, she was too miserable to dwell on anything but her discomfort. Aside from the blinding sun heating her exposed skin to what she was certain would be a wretched sunburn, the dry desert air parched her mouth and throat, and coarse pebbles had invaded the inside of the satin pumps, torturing her feet with every movement.

The veiled hat that went with her ensemble had never rested comfortably on her head, and now it bumped from side to side straining against the combs securing it. If not for the protection the veil afforded her face from the sun, Keeley would have tossed it entirely. As it was, her back was going to have a crisscross pattern from her shoulders to her waist from the satin spaghetti ribbons lacing the sides of the deep V together.

She was wondering darkly whether the sun would set before she collapsed, dehydrated, on the side of the road, at the mercy of a flock of vultures when a blaring horn startled her. Reflexively, she turned to the source of the racket.

It was the van Troy's friend Cork had rented. It slowed as it drew alongside her, and she stopped, ready to swallow her pride and climb aboard. Though there were certain parallels in the two potential situations that didn't escape her, an awkward drive with five people scowling at her couldn't be any worse than collapsing and being picked apart by buzzards.

But the van didn't stop. Suddenly, each of the long side windows was filled with the rounded cheeks of bare backsides pressed against the glass. As soon as her face registered shock, the vehicle took off with a spin of wheels that sent loose sand flying like debris on the edge of a twister. Keeley knew she could not possibly hear them jeering at her, since the discordant honking of the horn continued until the van was well past her, but ugly laughter echoed in her mind.

Mooned. She'd been mooned in broad daylight! As if she hadn't already been humiliated enough walking down the highway in a wedding dress that looked as if it had been bought at the Bordello Boutique!

Someday, she'd be angry.

Someday, this whole miserable episode might mellow into a funny anecdote to tell at parties.

But at this very moment, all Keeley wanted was to sit down right where she was and sob. And she would have done just that if she'd had any tears to shed. But a woman on the verge of dehydration couldn't risk depleting any of the moisture in her body. So she walked. And fumed.

Class whispers, lack of it shouts. One of her grandmother's old sayings suddenly came to mind. Her grandmother had an old saying to cover every situation, and that one certainly covered Troy and company's latest escapade.

I should have listened to Granny, Keeley thought. Granny had warned that nothing good would come from big cities and associating with wild city people. People like Troy Mitchell—outrageous, uninhibited, seize-the-moment Troy Mitchell. Handsome, charismatic and irreverent, he'd been the absolute embodiment of the freedom she'd always dreamed of while she'd sat on the porch swing back home, feeling cut off from the world beyond the Lakeside city limits.

Lost in thought, she stumbled as the pointed toe of her right shoe encountered the exposed top of a half-buried rock. Muttering a word that would have sent her granny in search of a bar of soap, she fought the combination of gravity, five-inch heels and unstable sand to regain her balance, narrowly avoiding a face-first tumble onto the sand.

And to think she'd always believed those hours in Miss Sylvie's School of Dance were a waste of time! Grimacing at the potential for bloody disaster she'd just averted, she shoved the veiled hat back onto the center of her head. Damn, but those dainty-looking plastic combs could yank hair. And she must have twisted her ankle during her aerial ballet, because it didn't feel any better than her scalp.

Granny was right—I'd have been better off staying in Lakeside, she decided. She could be sitting in that porch swing now, with her face turned into the breeze instead of in this godforsaken desert choking on the acrid stench of automobile exhaust while she limped toward the worst of what civilization had to offer.

This wasn't going to work. She moved past simple frustration to genuine desperation. Her heels sank every time she put her foot down, and the wrenched ankle made walking even more difficult.

Just as she realized that she desperately needed help, she was presented with a solution to her dilemma; not just one cab, but three in rapid succession, passed her, all traveling in the direction she needed to go.

Carrying tourists from the airport to the downtown hotels, of course. And there were bound to be others. All she had to do was stop one.

Keeley had never been in a taxi, much less hailed one, but she didn't see that as a major problem. She'd seen movies. You just raised your arm and shouted, "Taxi!" How hard could it be?

As she stood facing the oncoming traffic, waiting for a cab to come within range, her heels burrowed deeper into the sand. Seconds crawled at a snail's pace as she waited, but it wasn't too long before she spied a dome atop an approaching car. Thrusting her arm in the air, she called out, "Taxi!"

The vehicle sped past as though she were invisible. Disheartened, she released a weary sigh as that cab, too, disappeared into the horizon. She tried again a few minutes later, still unsuccessfully. Her jaw dropped in astonishment. She couldn't believe the drivers would leave a woman stranded alone on the side of the road.

The next taxi slowed enough for Keeley to catch sight of a child gawking at her from the back side window before resuming highway speed. *Better a child's face than an adult's behind,* she thought wryly. *Keeley Owens was coming up in the world.*

Yet another cab passed before her desperation gave way to pure, old-fashioned anger. Weren't taxis licensed and regulated? Didn't that give them some sort of civic responsibility to help people in trouble? There had to be some way to make them stop—

The hitchhiking scene from *It Happened One Night* popped into her mind as she yanked her heels from the sand and stepped closer to the highway. Although she had less skirt to work with than Claudette Colbert had had in the film, she still had a few inches of decency left. Working the hem of the skirt up her thigh, she contemplated that nothing sparked inspiration quite as well as desperation.

With the skirt hiked, she flashed her leg, thrust out her chest and smiled provocatively. The next driver slowed...long enough to get an eyeful and return her smile with a lecherous leer before saying something to the two tropical-shirted men ogling her from the back seat. Then he hit the accelerator with enough force to throw up a spray of sand.

That does it! Keeley thought bitterly, brushing the sand from her arms. By God, the next taxi that appeared on the horizon was going to stop, even if she had to resort to throwing her body in front of it!

DIGBY BARNES HAD second thoughts about his decision not to rent a car as he folded his long frame into the back seat of a taxi at the airport, but his doubts were fleeting. A driver's seat would have provided ample legroom, but it also would have required studying a map and fighting traffic. He hadn't tossed everything into a suitcase and fled Indianapolis on the spur of the moment to trade the frustration of not being able to fit a round peg into a square hole for the challenge of navigating a strange car through unfamiliar streets. He was here to distance himself from a vexing problem, to relax, to have some fun if it came his way, and to hope that a fresh perspective would prove productive when he returned to his workshop.

"Where to?" asked the driver.

"The Circus-Circus looks like a Las Vegas–type of place," Digby replied. Hopefully, they'd have a room. If not, he'd just go wherever the urge took him and see where he ended up.

"You got it," the driver said. Later, after they'd left the airport congestion for open highway, the man asked, "This your first time in Vegas?"

"Yep," Digby said.

"You come to gamble or see the shows?"

"I hadn't given it much thought."

"Most people do a little of both," the driver said, and Digby wondered how many times the man went through his repertoire of stock questions and observations each shift.

A few minutes later, the cab began to slow. "What the—?" the driver said. "Some broad's in the middle of the street, waving her arms."

Digby leaned forward to check out the view. The woman looked like a refugee from the set of low-budget movie. She was dressed in white from head to foot, including a hat with a veil. He would have guessed maybe it was a bridal outfit, but there was nothing chaste or virginal about the flared, ruffled skirt or the way the dress fell off her shoulders, exposing a lot of skin. If Digby had ever seen a dress that said, "Take me," this was it. "Who do you think it is?" he asked.

The driver snorted impatiently. "Some showgirl high on something."

"All the way out here?"

"See for yourself," the driver said, slowing the cab to a crawl.

Digby could not entirely believe what he was seeing, as the mystery woman in white hiked her skirt to the limit of common decency and kicked her right leg, Rockette-style. He couldn't see her face, but her manner suggested a painful reaction that aborted the kick at waist level—still enough to titillate the imagination.

Resolutely, she shifted and switched legs. This time, the kick reached shoulder level, but from the trouble she had maintaining her balance on one leg in the high heels she was wearing, it was obvious this was no showgirl. "She's no professional," he said, voicing his thought aloud.

"A wannabe," the driver said, tapping the horn a couple of times. "Probably fresh off the farm."

"She doesn't look like any farm girl I've ever seen," Digby said. *But whoever she was, the closer he got, the better she looked.*

Keeley was gratified almost to tears when the taxi slowed almost immediately. Satisfied that the cab could easily stop in time to avoid hitting her, she gave up her high kicks, strutted into the middle of the lane and, planting her hands on her hips, struck what she hoped was a seductive pose. She might be in Vegas, but this was no time to take chances. Others had slowed, but none had stopped.

As soon as the cab came to a complete halt, she dashed to the front passenger door as fast as a woman wearing spike heels could dash on heat-softened asphalt. Exuding gratitude, she grabbed the door handle, only to discover that the door was locked. The passenger-side front window, however, crept down, and the driver, a bald-headed man with a handlebar mustache, said, "I don't know what you're on, lady, but you could get killed dancing around in the road like that."

"On?" It took her a moment for his meaning to sink in. "I'm not *on* anything. I need a ride into town."

"No way, lady."

"But...you have to—"

"Lady, I don't have to do anything but pay taxes and die," he said. "You're two deuces short of a deck if you think I'm letting you in this cab."

"But—" *How could he even think of refusing to let her in the car?* "I don't have any other way—"

The end of the sentence was drowned out by the screech of brakes and the shrill wail of a horn as a pickup truck bore down on the taxi from behind and laid rubber on the road as it changed lanes to avoid a collision, missing the sedan by inches.

"You're going to get us killed, lady," the driver barked. "Now get away from the door so I don't drag you with me when I pull out." He accelerated slightly, forcing her to let go of the door handle or walk alongside the moving vehicle.

She took a few steps. "Please. I—"

Releasing a snort of impatience, the driver jammed the brakes and said, "Look, I'll radio the dispatcher to call a squad car for you, and you can do your explaining to the cops."

"But—"

"That's the best I can do," he snapped. "Even if I wanted to give you a ride, I couldn't. I already have a fare."

"Let her in."

Keeley and the driver both turned their heads to look at the passenger in the back seat. He was certainly large enough to live up to the authority of his voice, a broad-shouldered, wide-chested hulk of a man with a neck that could have won him a gig on a Marine Corps recruiting poster—and a face that would have earned him the job of drill sergeant.

"Are you kidding?" the driver said. "This could be a setup. She could be armed."

The passenger's brown eyes homed in on Keeley's face with the accuracy of a heat-seeking missile, giving Keeley the uncomfortable feeling that he hadn't missed a single beat of her performance. The lazy smile that lifted the corners of his mouth with almost negligent nonchalance reinforced the conviction, especially when he said, "I don't know where you think she could be concealing a weapon."

The cabbie chortled. "You're obviously not from Vegas."

The smile relaxed into an expression of mocking amusement at the driver. "I don't believe our distressed damsel is from Vegas, either. And I have a feeling the two of us could handle any mischief she tries to make."

The cabbie muttered something about yokels from Iowa or Kansas. Ignoring him, the man in the back seat unlocked the door, opened it and cocked an eyebrow at Keeley.

Keeley suddenly held little doubt that the man who'd just opened the door for her could have handled any mischief made by a well-trained team of special-forces paratroopers. He was a real "take charge" kind of guy. But at the moment, if Godzilla had been the one to open the door and lift a monstrous eyebrow in invitation, she would have gotten in that taxi, because it meant not having to slough her way through the sand any longer.

"There's a sucker born every minute," the driver muttered.

The man cast him a quelling look. "The lady is with me. Either she gets in, or I get out."

"Oh, what the hell?" the cabbie relented. "This is Vegas. We're supposed to live on the edge."

Climbing into the cool air in the vehicle was like stepping into heaven after a brief visit in hell. Keeley's sighed "Thank you" got lost in the roar of the engine as the driver, mumbling under his breath, hit the gas pedal. Coaxing the taxi to highway speeds, he asked over his shoulder, "You still wanna go to the Circus-Circus?"

"I don't know," her fellow passenger replied. "I'll ask the lady." Although he spoke to the driver, the full force of his gaze leveled on Keeley's face.

Oh, yes. He could handle a special-forces troop; this man could probably handle an entire army. Especially if the soldiers were women.

"Where do you want to go?" he asked.

"My hotel," she said. "I have to—" *Move out of Troy's*

room. "I need...clothes...shoes...my purse." *What's left of my self-esteem. What's left of my...life.*

"Which hotel?" the man asked with surprising gentleness.

Keeley told him, and he passed the information on to the driver. Keeley crossed one leg over the other and took off one shoe, reversed the action and removed the other one. Although she'd known the sand was chafing her skin, she gasped when she discovered patches of blood on the white lace stockings. Blinking back tears of frustration, she rolled down the window and shook the sand from each shoe in turn. Only years of strict training never, *never* to litter stopped her from tossing the damn things onto the side of the road. Instead, she held them with the relish she might have had for a three-day-old fish carcass while she buzzed the window closed, then dropped them haphazardly onto the floorboard next to her tortured feet.

The hat was next. This one, she did toss—into the front seat. "A souvenir," she told the driver sarcastically. She ran her hands through her hair a few times, massaging the tender areas where the combs had been, to reassure herself that she didn't have two bald spots, then leaned her head back, closed her eyes and sighed as her shoulders sagged into the stiff seat.

"You look like you could use something to drink," "Mr. Take Charge" observed.

"I would walk across hot coals for a glass of water," Keeley replied, not bothering to open her eyes.

"That won't be necessary," he said. Then she heard the sucking pop of a lid coming off a bottle. She opened her eyes to discover a bottle of water inches in front of her nose, held there by a hand the size of a grizzly bear's paw. The man's gaze fell to her feet. "It looks to me like you've already done the equivalent."

Oddly embarrassed that he'd seen the bloodstains on her stockings, she explained unnecessarily, "The, uh, sand got in my shoes."

"Those weren't exactly desert hiking boots you were wearing."

Keeley took a swallow of water. "I wasn't planning on hiking across the desert when I put them on."

"Obviously," he said, sliding his gaze upward to take in her legs. It settled on the stretch of thigh left uncovered by the miniskirt of her dress and lingered long enough to make Keeley self-conscious. There was a lot of pure virility in those sharp brown eyes.

Clearing her throat, she stared at the label on the bottle in her hand. "Do you always carry water around with you?"

"I usually throw a couple of bottles in my bag before I go on vacation. Since I fly standby, I never know how long I'll be hanging around the airport before I catch a flight."

"Standby? You don't buy tickets ahead of time?"

"Not when I'm traveling for fun."

"How do you plan your trip when you don't know when you'll be leaving or arriving?"

"The whole point of going on vacation is not having to plan," he said. "The fun is in not knowing what's going to happen next."

"You sound like—" *Troy*. She drew in a breath and released it. "Someone I used to know."

"This trip is a perfect example," he said. "When I left home this morning, I had no idea I was going to wind up in Las Vegas, in a cab with a beautiful woman."

"I didn't know I was going to end up stranded on the highway in a wedding dress from Fantasies 'R Us, either, but that doesn't make it fun."

He grinned unexpectedly. "I knew there was a story behind that wedding dress. What happened—you get stood up?"

"No!" Keeley snapped. "Of course not! I was the one—" Frowning, she paused to regroup her thoughts. "The whole thing was a bad idea."

"Anything involving wedding chapels usually is." He touched the base of her ring finger briefly. "I take it you came to that conclusion *before* the vows were exchanged."

"Yes," she said, adding under her breath, "Thank God."

"I heard that!" he teased.

Keeley frowned. "Troy isn't a bad person. He's just—"

"Your typical, insensitive male jerk?"

"Immature," Keeley said.

"Immature enough to leave a woman stranded in the desert, apparently."

"Thank you for pointing that out," she said irritably. *Why don't you just rub a little salt into the wounds?*

The man shrugged his shoulders. "Pardon me for noticing, but you were a little hard to ignore, doing the cancan in the middle of the highway."

Keeley took a cooling draft of water and reminded herself that this man had supplied the bottle from which she slaked her thirst. But she had to be fair to Troy. "I humiliated him," she said. "He was hurt, and angry."

"It never ceases to amaze me how quickly women

jump to the defense of men who treat them like the half-eaten Twinkie from yesterday's lunch box," the man said.

"That makes me feel *so* much better," Keeley said. *A half-eaten Twinkie! As if she hadn't felt bad enough already.*

"Here we are," the driver said, taking an abrupt right into the hotel's circular driveway. He stopped the cab at the front entrance and looked at the meter. "That'll be fourteen dollars." Then, hitting a lever as an afterthought, he added, "And a buck-fifty for the extra passenger."

Money.

One of life's little curveballs was heading her way again.

She stole a glance at "Take Charge." He was taking out his wallet. *If she played this right, she might avoid major embarrassment.*

Any more *major embarrassment.*

"Turn your head," she ordered.

"Hmm?"

Keeley spun her forefinger in the air. "Your head. Turn your head." Then she scowled at the driver, who was drumming his fingers on the dashboard impatiently. "You, too."

Satisfied that neither man was watching, she inched her hand under her skirt for the dollar bills she had tucked in the lace band of the thigh-highs. She never went anywhere without her emergency fund, what Granny had called "mad money." In case a girl got "mad" and had to get home on her own. *In case a girl ran out of a wedding chapel and wound up in the desert outside Las Vegas and had to hail a cab.*

Easily locating the neatly folded bills, she pulled them from under the bottom edge of her skirt. "You can..." Her voice trailed off as she caught her rescuer staring at her and enjoying what he was seeing. She exhaled gloomily and finished, "—look now."

Feeling her sunbaked cheeks growing even hotter in embarrassment, she offered him the stash. "Here's two dollars. That's all I have with me. But if you'll give me your business card, I'll mail you the rest of the fare."

Grinning, he pushed her hand—and the money—aside and peeled a twenty from his wallet. His eyes remained firmly fixed on Keeley's face as he thrust the bill at the driver. "I never take money from a woman," he said. "Especially cash. Somebody might think I'm a gigolo."

He certainly had all the necessary physical attributes for that job, Keeley thought. "But—"

"No arguments," he said, shaking his head and waving away the driver's offer of change. "It's done."

They stared at each other a moment. The memory of standing on the side of the road with her heels buried in the sand passed through Keeley's mind, bringing back the fear and desperation she'd been feeling before the cab had stopped. She swallowed. "Then...thank you."

"It was my pleasure," he said, the warmth in his eyes testament to his words.

A moment passed in silence. Keeley found herself smiling at her rescuer. Although she thought of his face as drill-sergeant severe, his features were not unpleasant, just...strong. In fact, he could almost be considered handsome, in a macho, blatantly virile kind of way.

"I...uh, have to get my shoes on," she said.

"Are you sure you want to put them on over those blisters?"

"It was the sand, not the shoes," she said, fighting the quiver in her chin. "I'm going to look ridiculous enough crossing that lobby in this outfit. I'm not going to go in there barefoot, as well."

"This is Las Vegas. You'll just be another colorful footnote for the tourists from Ohio."

"My life's ambition," she said. "Famous, though nameless, in Ohio."

"Come on. Chin up. You don't have to go in alone. I'll be with you."

"You don't have to go to all that trouble."

"It's no trouble. I have to go to the desk anyway. I'm checking in."

"Checking in? But...what about the Circus-Circus?"

"What about it?"

"I thought—"

"That I had reservations?" he asked, with a mocking lift of eyebrow. "I saw a poster for the Circus-Circus at the airport and it sounded like it had potential. But now I'm here, and this place seems even more promising. Besides, my mother taught me that a gentleman always walks a woman to her door to make sure she gets inside safely."

Keeley found the sensual glint in his brown eyes unnerving. "If you're hoping that I'm going to show my gratitude by—"

"As interesting as the idea may be, I assure you that it never occurred to me to try to *collect* on a kind act," he said curtly.

Keeley's cheeks flamed. She hadn't meant to insult him. She searched for the right words of apology.

"You two gonna get out, or sit and talk?" the driver

asked gruffly. "'Cause if you're going to sit here, I'm going to turn the meter back on."

"We're getting out," "Mr. Take Charge" said.

"Both of you?"

"Both of us."

"I'll get your suitcase," the driver grumbled, leaning over to release the trunk latch before getting out of the car.

"Mr. Take Charge" reached for the door handle to follow, but Keeley stopped him with a hand on his forearm. He looked at her curiously.

"I didn't mean to insult you," she said. "I'm not quite myself. I guess I overreacted. I just didn't want any...misunderstandings."

He mulled over the apology a moment before a cat-with-a-canary-feather-in-his-mouth smile slid over his face.

"I'll forgive the insult if you let me buy you a drink," he said, and Keeley had the distinct impression that she'd just been conned.

2

KEELEY HAD KNOWN her rescuer was large by the way he'd filled so much of the available space in the back seat of the taxi. But even as she watched him unfold from the car, she did not fully comprehend how big he was. It wasn't until he walked to her side of the car and she found herself craning her neck to see his face that she realized he was probably half an inch closer to seven foot than six.

It was going to be like walking through the lobby with a cross between the Incredible Hulk and the Jolly Green Giant—only not green. Between her dress and his size, they were going to be about as inconspicuous as an ostrich and a bull at a garden party. But he seemed determined to escort her in, and the bottom-line truth was, she did feel a measure of safety knowing she didn't have to risk running into Troy and his friends alone.

If he was the least bit self-conscious because of her outlandish dress, he didn't show it. With typical male disregard for such matters, he lifted an eyebrow in inquiry. "Ready?"

Keeley nodded and took a step, then winced as her weight shifted onto her right ankle.

His forehead crinkled. "You okay?"

"I stumbled on a rock," she said. "My ankle's a little

tender." Her blistered heels were killing her, too, but she refused to be a whiner.

"You can lean on me if you like."

Keeley shook her head. *No way was she going to lean on him.* With her luck, she'd enjoy it too much, and she didn't need that right now. "It's not even swollen. I'll be fine once I get these shoes off."

Except for a dozen or so people cranking slot machines, the lobby was deserted. She and her marine crossed to the desk and approached separate clerks. Keeley identified herself to the woman helping her, asked for a key to the room in which she had been staying with Troy and explained that she wanted to check into a single room in her own name.

The clerk typed something into the computer and looked from the monitor to Keeley. Her eyes narrowed as she gave Keeley a questioning appraisal. "What did you say your name is?"

"Owens. Keeley Owens."

"I show a K. Owens as staying in the room, but you're not the primary registrant."

"That would be Troy," Keeley said. "He and I are...*were*...traveling together, but..." Her voice trailed off in a sigh and she drew a deep breath before starting over. "I've decided to move into a room of my own."

The clerk slid a registration form across the counter. "Would you fill this out, please."

As Keeley wrote her name and address on the form, she caught sight of her desert rescuer doing the same thing a few feet down the counter. She hurried, hoping to finish ahead of him and make a clean break to the elevators before he had a chance to mention the drink he'd wanted to buy her. She just wanted to get her things, take a leisurely bath and put the whole episode behind her. Including her rescuer, as appealing as he might be.

"Will you be securing the room with cash or a credit card?" the clerk asked.

"Credit card," Keeley said.

The clerk looked at her expectantly, finally prompting, "I'll need the card to make an imprint."

Keeley smiled and gave a slight shrug. "I'll have to bring it down later. My purse is up in the room."

"I'll need to see some kind of identification," the clerk said crisply. "A driver's license or other photo ID with a signature."

"Everything's up in the room," Keeley said.

The clerk's features firmed into an expression of authority. "I'm afraid that could be a bit of a problem. I can't check you into a room without some type of security deposit, and I couldn't possibly let you into Mr. Mitchell's room without some sort of identification."

"But it's my room, too!" Keeley argued. "My name is in the computer. You said so."

"It's a matter of policy," the clerk said. "Without photo ID, I have no way of knowing if you're K. Owens."

"Look," Keeley said, hysteria rising in her voice. "All you have to do is give me the key, and I'll be back in minutes with a whole fistful of ID and credit cards."

"It's a matter of policy," the clerk repeated. "The security measures at this hotel are among the strictest in the world."

"Then have security go with me and let me in," Keeley suggested. "I'll get my purse and show them my ID."

"I'm sorry. That's out of the question."

Keeley felt as though she'd scaled fences and forded streams only to encounter an unyielding brick wall.

"Where is Mr. Mitchell?" the clerk asked, trying to be helpful. "He could let you in the room."

"I was hoping to avoid Mr. Mitchell," Keeley replied sharply.

Female-to-female understanding flashed in the clerk's eyes. "I'm sorry. But there's nothing I can do."

"Who *could* do something?" Keeley asked. "There has to be someone who could—"

"Are you having a problem..." It was "Mr. Take Charge". Riding to her rescue again. Keeley saw his gaze slide to the registration card on the other side of the counter before he finished pointedly, "*Keeley?*"

Caught between hope and aggravation, Keeley tensed involuntarily and said, "It's nothing. Just—" She forced a laugh, as though the situation were a minor annoyance instead of the disaster it really was. "My purse and credit cards are up in the room, and I don't have my key, so I can't check in yet."

He tossed his own credit card across the counter to the clerk. "Check Miss—" his eyes swept over the registration card again "—*Owens* into a room."

"You don't have to...I couldn't let—"

"I insist," he said.

The clerk picked up the card.

"Don't use that," Keeley said.

"Aw, come on, Keeley," he said. "I know you're miffed about your vacation getting ruined, but you know your father would have my job if I left you stranded in the lobby."

"My father?" Keeley pushed the words through clenched teeth.

"You know how the senator gets when he thinks you're in danger."

"Senator?" Keeley mouthed. *What in the world was this lunatic up to?*

"In danger?" the desk clerk asked.

Oozing male charisma, Take Charge addressed the clerk. "Senator Owens. Republican. Indiana. The Senator Owens who is vice chairman of the House Subcommittee on Domestic Terrorism. Unfortunately, he and his fellow committee members have gotten a little too close to a faction of militant radicals, and there was a fax of some kind, with vague threats against the families of all the committee. It's probably nothing, but Senator Owens thought it might be better if his daughter wasn't diddly-bopping all over Las Vegas without any...protection."

Outraged by his gall, Keeley scowled at him. Undaunted, he grinned. "I know I promised to be as inconspicuous as possible, but I can't leave you in the lobby." He addressed the clerk. "Go ahead and check Miss Owens in on this card. When she gets ready to check out, she can give you her own card. In the interim, she'll be comfortable and...*safe*."

"Safe?" the clerk repeated.

He nodded.

"From terrorists?"

He nodded again.

The clerk cleared her throat. "I see. Well, Mr....Barnes," she said, reading his name before sliding the card through the scanner. "I guess, under the circumstances, we should get her checked in immediately. May I have your key folder, please?"

"Certainly," he said, winking as he handed it across the counter.

He *winked* at the desk clerk! Keeley couldn't believe it. The man was shamelessly manipulative. And what was worse, Keeley was sure that he usually got away with it because he was so...well, the way he was!

The clerk furiously punched keys on the computer keyboard then stared at the monitor, waiting for some information to come up. When it did, her face brightened as though she'd just thought up the solution to a world crisis. She removed the plastic key from "Mr. Take Charge's" folder and replaced it with a new one. Then she marked through the room number and wrote a new number above the strikeout before preparing a similar folder for Keeley. Holding one in each hand, she offered them the new folders. "Thank you. I'm sorry about the problem earlier. We do have policies."

"We're all squared away now," the man said, with a smug grin. "We'll be sure to tell Miss Owens's father how helpful you were. Right, Keeley?"

"That would be...Senator Owens?" the clerk asked.

"He'll be most appreciative for your help," the man said, bending to pick up his suitcase.

Unable to tolerate another second of the farce, Keeley took off at a trot for the elevators. Her rescuer caught up with her just as the elevator arrived and they both stepped into the car and reached for the elevator buttons at the same time. He gestured for her to push her button first. She pressed six.

"Me, too," he said.

"It figures," Keeley said. Then she added, "She

didn't swallow a word of that cockamamy story, you know."

He shrugged. "It got the job done."

Keeley appreciated his sharing the cab, but her ankle was throbbing, her heels were burning, her heart ached and her ego was shattered. She had no energy or patience left for the kind of tomfoolery he'd pulled at the desk. She folded her arms across her waist. *How long could it take an elevator to climb six floors?* "Doesn't it bother you at all that you lied through your teeth?"

"It was a harmless little lie. No one got hurt or cheated, and you got a room. Isn't that what you wanted?"

"I'm going to take them my card as soon as I get my things."

"I know that. That's why it seemed ridiculous for you to be sitting in the lobby all mussed up and miserable when you could be in a room relaxing."

"I guess I owe you another thank-you," she said. "But that doesn't make me approve of your methods."

"Your gratitude is acknowledged and accepted... along with your disapproval."

The elevator stopped abruptly and the fourth-floor light beamed on. The doors opened to a man wearing a bathing suit with a towel slung over his shoulder, obviously on his way to the rooftop pool. Impulsively, Keeley stepped out of the car. Troy's room was on the fourth floor. She might as well see if he was there. Since the hotel obviously wasn't going to let her into the room, she was going to have to get in through Troy's benevolence. If she faced him now, at least she'd have some clothes to change into after she washed off the dust.

She didn't realize he'd followed her until the doors were already closing. "This isn't the sixth floor," she said.

"I know that," he said. "So where are we going?"

"*We* are not going anywhere," she said. "There is no *we.*" *Another place, another time, other circumstances, maybe. But not here. Not now.* "*You* are going to catch the next car up to your room. *I* am going to try to get my things."

"I thought you might need some moral support."

Need, yes. Want, no. "Look, I appreciate everything you've done, but...enough is enough."

Scowling, he grumbled, "Try to be a nice guy—"

"Why don't you just...go to your room!" She turned around and punched the up button then started down the hall, walking with as much *hauteur* as the spike heels and her tender ankle would allow.

She knocked at Troy's door several times, but she wasn't surprised when no one answered. He and the rest of the gang were probably hitting every bar and casino between the chapel and the hotel. There was no way to predict when they might show up again. All she could do was leave a message for him at the desk and call the room periodically to try to catch him in.

Disheartened, she limped back to the elevator.

If her rescuer had still been there, she would have let him carry her to her room.

THE FIRST THING Digby noticed was the door connecting his room to the adjacent one. Actually, there were two doors, one facing each room, either of which could be locked or unlocked only from one side. In essence, when both doors were open, the neighboring rooms became a suite; when either or both were closed, each room functioned as a singular unit.

The door on his side was slightly ajar, and curiosity led him to check the one facing the adjoining room. It, too, was about an inch ajar, and a quick scan told him the other room was as yet unoccupied.

But not for long, he speculated. An involuntary grin tugged at the corners of his mouth. He'd thought it was odd that the desk clerk had changed his room assignment just because he'd guaranteed another room. He'd be willing to bet the casino that a certain brunette would be arriving momentarily.

Unless she and the groom she didn't marry took one look at each other and decided to make up.

That thought was enough to wipe the grin from his face. If she made up with the boyfriend, it was going to drop a monkey wrench in his plans. The moment he'd taken in that absurd cancan she was doing in the middle of the road, he'd decided that *she* was going to be his vacation.

He unpacked his clothes and tossed his shaving kit onto the vanity, worked off his shoes and stretched out on the bed with his shoulders propped on two pillows, anticipating Keeley's arrival.

He didn't have to wait long. A scant minute passed before he heard someone enter the adjoining room, slamming the door behind her. Two thumps followed in rapid succession, accompanied by a grumbled expletive. *That would be the shoes.*

Again he waited, silently counting seconds until she noticed the door linking her room to his. Twenty, twenty-one, twenty-two—

"No way!" Miss Keeley Owens's face appeared in the doorway.

Until he saw her eyes narrow, her chin jut and her nostrils flare, Digby had never been inspired to put voice to the movie cliché by telling a woman that she was beautiful when she was angry. Biting back the observation, which he knew from watching old movies would only add fuel to the fire, he flashed her what he hoped was a charming grin as he sat up and dropped his feet to the floor. "It came as a total surprise to me, too."

"Oh, right! Like you didn't wink at the desk clerk."

Digby stood up. *She'd noticed that he'd winked at the desk clerk!* He took it as a positive sign. Encouraged, he stepped in her direction. "Did you rendezvous with Mr. Wonderful?"

"No." Her scowl deepened as she crossed her arms in front of her. "Not that it's any of your business."

"I *did* rescue you after he left you stranded." *It couldn't hurt to keep reminding her what a louse the ex-fiancé was. And what a knight he, Digby Barnes, had been.*

"You gave me a ride," she said, "not CPR."

Digby grinned. "If I'd known you wanted mouth-to-mouth, I'd have been happy to oblige."

"You're a real Boy Scout!" she said sarcastically.

"Ingrate!" Digby teased.

She chewed on her bottom lip as she mulled that over. Digby thought that he wouldn't mind chewing on the lip for her, but he refrained from offering.

"I'm locking the door on my side," she announced at last. Her chin tilted up in a gesture of defiance that wasn't reflected in the rest of her face. But her features created a fascinating canvas of emotion. And her eyes flashed a blend of fear, confusion and vulnerability that made him want to pull her into his arms and protect her.

Digby shrugged as if the matter was of little significance to him. "Suit yourself. But I'm here in case—"

"You are not *obligated* to take care of me," she said. "This isn't some ancient Oriental culture where if you save a person's life you're responsible for her forever...not that you actually saved my life."

"A man has a right to be concerned about a fellow human being in any culture," he said. "You've obviously been through a lot today. I'm just trying to be helpful."

She let out a weary sigh. "It's not that I don't appreciate what you did, but—"

"Just knock if you need anything."

Scowling, she stepped back and began pushing the door closed.

"You know how to knock, don't you?" Digby said. "You just curl your hand into a fist and—"

"When hell freezes over!" filtered through the sturdy door.

Digby laughed as the bolt shot home with a loud clunk. *We'll just see about that, Miss Keeley Owens. We'll just see.*

3

KEELEY LEANED against the bolted door feeling as though someone had drained all the energy from her. The beast! He was laughing at her. Anyone with an ounce of sense instead of a pound of testosterone would realize that a woman who'd been through what she'd been through today would want only two things—a tub of warm water and solitude.

She wouldn't turn down a change of clean clothes, either. Once she got out of this horrid farce of a wedding dress, she was throwing it in the trash. Which meant that she was going to have to wear a towel or fashion a toga from a bedsheet.

Thinking longingly of the scented shower gel in her makeup bag in the room two floors below, she peeled herself off the door to check out the toiletries the hotel offered. She was halfway to the bathroom when "Mr. Take Charge" knocked at the adjoining door. She stopped and turned, but didn't answer.

"Keeley?" he called, adding another bout of rigorous thunking. "I know you can hear me."

"I'm ignoring you."

"You don't want to do that," he said in a smug, taunting tone.

Keeley remained stubbornly silent.

"Okay. Have it your way. But I have some things you might find useful."

Hating herself for allowing him to bait her, Keeley clenched her teeth to keep from speaking and waited for him to go on.

"I have a T-shirt you could borrow. It would be big on you, but it's clean, and it would be more comfortable than that garb you had on."

Keeley grimaced. A clean shirt! The idea was so appealing that declining the offer inflicted emotional pain. But she couldn't cave. She couldn't let herself be had so easily. But, oh, the thought of that shirt—

Maybe if he persisted just a little longer—

"Keeley?" He knocked again. "I'm going to put it on the floor between the two doors and then lock my door, in case you change your mind. Okay?"

Keeley ran to the door and pressed her ear against it.

"This is me, closing the door," he said.

She heard the click of the door closing, the clunk of the bolt engaging. He couldn't fake that, could he? She gave it close to a minute before gingerly turning the bolt that released the door on her side. Halfway expecting him to spring at her like a jack-in-the-box, she grabbed the shirt. As she lifted it, something hard fell out, hitting the floor with a thump. A hairbrush.

She scooped it up, shoved the door closed with her hip and bolted it. "Thanks," she said, almost choking on the word.

"You're welcome," he said. Smugly.

Damn his conniving hide! He knew just how to make a woman an offer she couldn't refuse.

Determined to forget him and every other conniving, manipulative, insensitive, obnoxious, conceited, arrogant, self-centered male on the face of the earth for a few minutes, she limped to the bathroom and started filling the tub, then peeled the blood-encrusted stockings from her feet. Her chafed heels stung when she first lowered them into the water, but after a few seconds of agony, the stinging eased and she began to relax. The hotel's facial soap wasn't bubble bath, but it was creamy and smelled clean and slightly floral.

Sliding down until her neck rested comfortably on the rim of the tub, she closed her eyes. As the water went from soothingly warm, to tepid, to cool, the events of the day cascaded through her mind like reruns of an old *Twilight Zone* episode.

They had come on a five-day excursion package—Keeley and Troy, Troy's best friend, Brian, and the woman he'd been living with for the past six months, and a former roommate of Troy and Brian's who went by the unlikely nickname of Cork.

Keeley had never felt comfortable around Cork, who had a hard time keeping his hands to himself and who had a penchant for brainless women with big hair and hefty chests. He'd brought along his flavor of the week in the form of Suzzi, who'd complained about everything from the time the plane was scheduled to take off, to the width of the airline seats, to the food they were served on the plane and the color of the van they were assigned by the rental agency.

The only thing that seemed to have met Suzzi's approval on the entire trip, Keeley reflected bitterly, *had been Troy*. She'd fawned over him from the moment Cork had made introductions at the airport gate.

The day had started out normally. They'd all slept until ten and met for an early lunch, after which the men—and Suzzi—had been chomping at the bit to break their bills into change and hit the slot machines.

Keeley wasn't surprised when Troy became a maniac as soon as he started dropping coins into the one-armed bandits. Troy never did anything halfway or halfheartedly.

Except when it came to *me*, Keeley thought bitterly. He'd been happy enough to have her sharing his apartment. He liked a woman in his bed and he wasn't averse to a woman in the kitchen because his appetite for good food was as hearty as his appetite for sex.

But he hadn't wanted a wife. He'd skirted the issue whenever possible and nixed the entire idea when she forced him to talk about it. *Oh, Troy, how did we let it get to this point before we faced the fact that it was over?*

Troy was the first truly charismatic man Keeley had ever known. She'd been attracted to his good looks, his devil-may-care attitude, his wildness and derring-do—much the way Suzzi had been attracted to him at the airport. The way most women were when they met Troy.

Flattered that he had selected her, Keeley had embraced her role as Troy's woman. Having grown up in a town where a grease fire at the local Burger Hut was considered breaking news and people still remembered that the mayor's wife had once had an affair with the assistant chief of police, she'd been awed when Troy introduced her to Church Street and Pleasure Island and trendy sports bars where he and his friends partied and hung out.

Lately, though, the novelty of that life-style had worn off for her. But not for Troy. To him, the slot machines had been the big package under the Christmas tree. He'd been dropping quarters into them for over twenty minutes when Keeley had began to fear that the two hundred dollars they'd earmarked for gambling wouldn't last until sundown. She'd tactfully suggested that Troy slow down a little.

He'd less than tactfully suggested that she quit nagging.

Then he'd dropped in four quarters and pulled the bandit's arm, and all hell had broken loose. Coins poured from the machine, falling like flash-flood waters. Bells rang. Buzzers buzzed. Beefy security guards appeared from all directions to control the gathering crowd. The manager of the casino showed up to shake Troy's hand while his assistant took photos.

In all, Troy had won just over five thousand dollars. Complimentary drinks in one of the casino lounges had kicked off their celebration and, as he had more and more frequently in recent months, Troy had downed too many drinks, too quickly. The more he drank, the more boisterous and expansive he had become, grabbing Keeley for clumsy celebratory kisses and announcing that he had to do something spectacular to commemorate his good fortune.

"This is Vegas," Brian quipped. "Why don't you and Keeley tie the knot?"

Cork had almost choked on his beer laughing. "That's one thing you'd never forget!"

Troy had surprised them all by embracing the idea, probably because of the sheer outrageousness of it. Keeley had resisted at first, knowing deep in her heart that it wasn't what Troy really wanted. But Troy could be the most persuasive man in the world when he set his mind to it. Didn't she love him? Wasn't she always saying she wanted to get married? Why balk when they were in the perfect place for it?

It's just a damned good thing he never got it in his head to rob a bank and get me to pass the note to the teller, Keeley thought bitterly as she opened the drain of the tub. *I could have ended up sending Granny postcards from the federal penitentiary.*

Not that she would ever have robbed a bank—anymore than she'd ever marry a man on the spur of the moment knowing he didn't really want to marry her. At least not for any of the reasons a man should marry a woman.

She truly believed that Troy loved her as much as he could love anyone. The problem was, Troy loved himself too much to have much love left over for anyone else.

She drew the curtain and started the shower to shampoo her hair. She couldn't even muster up any righteous anger at Troy for leaving her in the desert. She understood him too well for that. He'd been hurt, and she'd humiliated him. He wasn't being deliberately mean, he was just insensitive to anything but his own needs. And one of his primary needs was the protection of his ego which, though large as a mountain, was fragile as a lightbulb. He hadn't been *abandoning* her, he'd been escaping an intolerable situation.

He'd been being Troy. Which was why she'd loved him—and why she couldn't marry him. And that's why she felt all empty inside. She should be crying, or raging, but she was just...numb.

She was almost relieved when pain stabbed up her leg as she stepped from the tub and unthinkingly put her full weight on her tender ankle. If not for the pain, she might wonder if she was even alive. She certainly appeared ghostly enough in the steam-fogged mirror above the sink, she thought, towel-drying her hair.

Before pulling her rescuer's T-shirt over her head, she unfolded it and studied it closely. Like its owner, it was enormous, a Chicago Bulls shirt that must have seen the inside of a washing machine at least a hundred times. Only a hint of scarlet tint indicated that it had probably once been bright red, and the black lettering had paled to a charcoal gray.

She pulled it on and the wear-softened cotton settled over her like a caress. The stretched-out hem ruffled her knees. For a moment she hugged herself, stroking the sleeves over her upper arms as though she were adjusting a new layer of skin. How wonderful it would be to wrap herself up in a cocoon and stay there, like a caterpillar, warm and cozy, until she felt whole and beautiful and ready to fly.

Cocoons? Caterpillars?

"You've lost it," she told her reflection, clearing now that she'd opened the door to let the steam out of the small bathroom. "You've really lost it."

After finger-combing her hair, she used her rescuer's brush to coax it into a passable style that would dry well. Keeley counted good hair at the top of her list of natural-beauty blessings. Her hair was a rich, glossy brown with a natural wave. In high school, she'd worn it waist-length, with the top and sides barretted. Now it was shoulder-length, layered and subtly highlighted with gold streaks.

Just knowing that she was stuck in her room until she could get real clothes and valid credit cards back in her possession made her restless. In a burst of impatience, she dialed Troy's room, but no one answered.

Discouraged, she hung up, wondering what she was supposed to do until someone answered the phone.

Why was it that a person always seemed to have either too little time or too much? Here she was with a four-day weekend, and she couldn't enjoy it. When she got back to work, with the Halloween rush breathing down her neck and the holidays soon to follow, she'd dream about idle hours. But right now, the minutes crawled. Right now, ringing phones to answer, stock catalogs to go through, order forms and employee schedules to fill out, boxes to open, merchandise to inventory and shelves to stock would be a godsend, diverting her attention from the fact that her personal life had just fallen apart.

She looked around the room without any interest in the flamboyant Vegas decor. The burnt orange-to-red color scheme failed to defeat the generic hotel-room ambience that included a quilted bedspread, wall-mounted bedside lamps, a built-in desk and a small round table that could be used for eating or playing cards at. A cardboard table-tent on the television promoted pay-for-view movies, and a plastic binder held information about the hotel's various dining rooms, casinos, pools and shops.

A quick surf through the channels yielded nothing more than reruns of *Gilligan's Island* and *Banacek*, a talk show featuring women who were breaking up with men who couldn't commit—wasn't that *just* what she needed?—and tips on being a better casino player. She muted the television and checked the listings of movies available through pay-for-view and found a choice of a superhero-saves-the-world-with-an-Uzi epic and something called *Mariah's Hot Dream Date,* which was accompanied by a stern warning that it contained explicit sexual situations and profanity.

Disgusted, she switched off the television, flopped onto the bed and let out a groan of sheer frustration. Two floors down, in the side pocket of her suitcase, there was a great romantic suspense novel by her favorite writer that she'd been wanting to read for months.

She would have pressed her face in the pillow and let out a bloodcurdling scream if she wasn't afraid she would be tempted to smother herself!

Stretching out, she plumped the pillow under her neck and tried to get comfortable. If she could only fall asleep, maybe Troy would be back in his room by the time she woke up. But she couldn't get comfortable. She turned one way and her ankle throbbed. She shifted until her ankle was comfortable and her chafed heel pressed against the bedding.

She couldn't close her eyes without seeing Troy standing next to her in that awful chapel, so drunk he was swaying on his feet, and then she'd relive that painful, disappointing moment of epiphany when she'd realized that she couldn't marry Troy because Troy didn't want to be married. The rest followed: running from the chapel; thinking Troy and his friends were stopping for her; the humiliation of becoming the target of their crude gesture of contempt; feeling alone, abandoned and scared. Desperation and humiliation were still close to the surface.

Her thoughts shifted to the man in the next room. The man whose shirt she was wearing, whose brush she'd used to style her hair, whose credit card had guaranteed her room. The man who, judging from the sounds filtering through the wall, was watching a football game on television. She might not appreciate his methods, but she owed him. If not for him, she'd still be downstairs in Troy's vision of the perfect wedding dress, with her feet still stuffed into those spike-heeled instruments of torture Troy had insisted were essential to the ensemble. For all she knew, she might still be wandering through the desert, or being treated for heat prostration at a hospital emergency room.

She'd have to write her rescuer a nice thank-you note and leave it for him at the desk. She searched the drawer at the built-in desk for hotel stationery. She couldn't leave the room dressed the way she was, so she might as well take care of the note while she was sitting around waiting for Troy to get back.

Dear—

Dear *who?* It was hard to write a note straight from the heart when you didn't know the name of the person to whom you were writing. She should have looked at his credit card when he secured the room, but she'd been too agitated to think about it. She drummed the desk top with the cheap plastic pen, contemplating how to open the letter. She could hardly address him as Dear "Mr. Take Charge."

Dear Rescuing Knight? Hardly! *Handsome Stranger?* Now *there* was a brilliant idea. *Good Samaritan?* Finally, deciding on "Nice, Helpful Stranger," she finished the salutation.

Thank you for—

She stopped abruptly when three firm knocks sounded on the door, followed closely by a deep voice. "Keeley?"

She put down the pen and turned toward the door.

She'd always heard that if you spoke of the devil, he would appear. Apparently, the same was true if you *wrote* of him.

"I know you're in there, Keeley."

"What is it?" She was already wearing his shirt— what more did he want?

"I have something in my room you might be interested in."

"I doubt that!" she said, although she knew she didn't. If only the circumstances had been different...

"I have cold drinks," he said. "Wine and cola. I ordered both since I didn't know which you'd prefer."

He paused, and Keeley had the uncomfortable feeling that he knew she was suddenly aware of how thirsty she was.

"There's food, too. Finger sandwiches and fruit. Melon," he said. "There's nothing better than melon on a hot day."

She would have been salivating like Pavlov's dog if she hadn't been so parched. Frowning, she stalked across the room, landing so heavily on her sore ankle that she gasped in pain as she turned the lock and flung open the door. "You don't play fair."

His face registered surprise before cracking into a sly smile. "I play to win. But I didn't know we had a game going. I just thought you might be hungry and thirsty after your adventure in the desert."

"You thought right," she said grudgingly. "I didn't realize it until you mentioned food, but I *am* famished."

"Dry heat takes it out of you," he said. His eyes slid from her face down her body, not missing a single detail. "I see the shirt...works."

Keeley smoothed the shirt self-consciously. "Yes. Thank you. It was thoughtful of you to offer it."

"I always said that was my lucky shirt."

"What's lucky about it?"

He chuckled. "Other than that it probably thinks it's died and gone to heaven?" He cocked an eyebrow sensuously and his voice turned husky. "I know I would."

"I can't do this," she said abruptly. "I appreciate all you've done, but I can't...I'm not up to this kind of thing." She turned to leave, but he stopped her, curving his fingers loosely over her shoulder.

"Please stay." His hand was large, but his touch was light. As soon as she stopped, he dropped his arm. "I didn't mean to make you uncomfortable. I wasn't making a pass."

"It's been a hell of a day," she said. "I'm overreacting to everything. I'm just not up to...socializing."

"You don't have to socialize. You don't have to say a thing." He gestured to the chair at the small table. "Just have something cold to drink and get some protein in your system. You'll feel better."

"What are you," she grumbled, limping to the chair, "a doctor?"

"Not even close," he said. "But I could probably manage to tape that ankle for you. But first things first...bottled water, cola or white wine?"

"Wine," she said, eyeing the bottles half-submerged in a bucket of ice. "But I've got to tell you—if you're hoping to get me blitzed, it's going to take a lot more than two of those little bottles."

"It never occurred to me to try to get you blitzed," he said in a wry tone that made her feel foolish for suggesting it. "Relaxed, maybe."

She smiled. "Relaxed would be nice."

He opened the bottle and passed it to her. "Go for it."

She was aware of him watching her like a concerned nanny as she lifted the drink to her lips, his solicitousness peculiarly at odds with his size and the severity of his features. She downed a sip and set the bottle on the table in front of her.

He thrust a platter of sandwiches in her direction. "Those little bagels with cream cheese are delicious."

"I'll try one," she said, lifting it from the plate to put it on her own. "What's in the cream puffs?"

"I haven't tried those yet," he said. "Guess I'm more of a bagel man."

Or leg-of-something-huge, she thought, involuntarily picturing him as a caveman hovering near a fire, ready to rip a quarter from the animal roasting there. She picked up a puff and ate it, then washed it down with wine. "Chicken salad with celery and walnuts," she reported, reaching for another.

He centered the platter on the table within easy reach of both of them. "I'll stick with the bagels."

"Most men like chicken," she observed.

"Chicken. Not chicken salad. I prefer to bite into my meat instead of having it chopped into unidentifiable pieces."

Keeley fought back the smile tugging at her lips as the image of her rescuer, done up in Alley-Oop fur overalls and wielding a leg of roast pterodactyl sprang to mind. "We haven't really met," she said. "I don't know your name."

"It's Digby."

"Digby?"

"It's an old family name," he explained. "My great-grandfather's name was Digby."

"That's nice," she said wistfully. "My mother saw the name Keeley in a magazine when she was carrying me. Of course, my great-grandmother's name was Pansy. I wouldn't have wanted to go through life with that one."

"Especially high school," he agreed. "So, Keeley, what do you do—aside from leaving men heartbroken at the altar?"

"*Heartbroken* is a bit of a stretch," Keeley said. "I suspect Troy's ego was more battered than his heart. But, in answer to your question, I run a party store."

"Where people buy crepe paper and stuff?"

"Crepe paper, banners, ribbons, balloons, party favors, confetti, umbrellas, plastic storks, centerpieces and yard signs. We also book party talent."

"What kind of talent?"

"Deejays, waiters, ponies, clowns, magicians, singing telegrams—whatever anybody wants. If someone wants something unique, we work with them."

"So how does one get into the party-store business?"

"I applied for a job. They needed a clown, and I needed the money. So I worked my way through college making balloon sculptures at children's birthday parties and store openings...and filling in at the store doing anything that needed doing. Once, I dressed up in a gorilla suit and sang "Let's Quit Monkeying Around and Get Hitched" when a customer was looking for a unique way to propose."

"I'm not familiar with that song—can you hum a few bars?"

"Only for prospective customers," she countered. "Are you planning on proposing to someone soon?"

Digby choked on the wine he'd just tipped into his mouth and wheezed, "No."

Keeley rolled her eyes in feigned exasperation. "So many men, so little commitment."

He rolled his eyes, mimicking her. "So many women, so few worth making a commitment to."

"Let's not start exchanging war stories," Keeley said, picking up her spoon to dig into the parfait glass of melon balls. "What's your line of work?"

"I tinker," he said.

"Tinker?"

"I'm a tinkerer. I invent things."

"What kind of things?"

"Whatever needs inventing."

"Like a story about my father being a senator?"

"That was an impromptu fabrication, not an invention."

"It was a con job," Keeley said drolly.

"It saved your butt."

Keeley frowned and reached for another sandwich. *The man was a flake, obviously. All* the promising ones were flakes. Or con men. "Can you make a living tinkering?"

"I get by," he answered nonchalantly. "People are usually willing to pay for something if they need it badly enough."

Keeley decided not to press for details she'd rather not know. She knew he was a con man; he could just as easily be a master forger or blackmailer. Trying not to show her impatience to be away from him, she finished her meal as quickly as possible, then thanked him abruptly and rose to leave.

"What's your hurry? I thought we were going to tape that ankle," he said.

"It's not bad," she lied. In fact, it was feeling worse than ever. "I...uh, need to try to call Troy again so I can get my things."

"Use my phone while I get the tape," he said. "It won't take but a minute to stabilize that ankle."

He seemed agreeable to her leaving once he'd administered first aid, and she didn't want to appear ungracious after all he'd done for her, so she nodded. She sat back down and reached for the phone.

"Still not there?" Digby said, returning from the bathroom as she slammed the phone down after letting it ring a dozen times.

"God only knows what bar or casino he's in."

As Digby knelt in front of her, Keeley suddenly became aware of the logistics of having a man examine her ankle when she was wearing his shirt and nothing else. She pressed her knees tightly together and lifted her foot. If he had anything in mind besides first aid—like the Sharon Stone interrogation scene from *Fatal Instinct*—he didn't show it. Settling her foot atop his thigh, he palpated the ankle with surprising efficiency.

"Nothing seems to be floating around," he said, tilting his head back to flash her a smile. "The prognosis is excellent. You're going to live."

"Like I was worried," Keeley grumbled.

"You keep up that sour attitude, and you're not going to get a lollipop," he said, picking at the end of the tape so he could peel off a strip.

"Excuse me if I'm not a model patient, but a twisted ankle is the least of my troubles at the moment."

"Are you having second thoughts about backing out of the wedding?"

"No," Keeley said, surprised at how easily the answer came, and how certain she was that she had done the right thing. "Troy and I had a lot of fun together, but it was over, even before we walked into the chapel."

"If that's the case, then it's probably better that it ended before it got too complicated."

"Yes. I—" She stopped abruptly, letting the thought trail into a sigh when she realized she was talking, virtually, to a stranger. A *flaky* stranger. "You're right. It would have been a lot more complicated if we'd gotten married and then found out it wasn't going to work."

"Let me know if I get this too tight," he said, winding the tape across and under her foot and up and behind her ankle in a figure eight. "The object is to stabilize, not cut off the circulation."

"It's not too tight," she said. "Where did you learn to do this, anyway?" *If he told her he'd been a Boy Scout, she was going to wallop him over the head with something.*

"I picked it up playing football."

"You're a football player?"

"I played in school," he said. "When you're six feet tall and husky in the sixth grade, people take it for granted that you're going to play football. There." He patted the top of her foot. "All done."

She stood up, testing her weight on the ankle. "That's much better. Thank—" her eyes locked with his, and followed them as he straightened to full height "—you."

She didn't just observe the sensual glint that came

into his eyes, she felt it. And she responded to it. Swiftly. Intensely.

I don't need this! she thought, frantically averting her gaze. It was just some weird physical anomaly brought on by stress. It had to be. She'd been standing in a wedding chapel with Troy only a few hours ago; she couldn't be attracted to another man now.

The moment passed. It passed slowly, but it passed. Digby seemed as nonplussed as Keeley by what had sparked between them. "I...uh, avoided putting tape on your heels. They're pretty raw."

"The sand," she said.

"Sand's very abrasive. That's...uh, why they make sandpaper out of it." He drew in a deep breath and exhaled before saying, "You really should put some antibiotic cream on them. I'll get it."

She followed him to within a few feet of the bathroom. "Do you always carry tape and antibiotic cream with you when you travel?" *Along with bottled water—even when you don't know where you're going?*

"Tinkering is a hands-on business," he said from inside the bathroom. He quickly returned with a tube of salve in hand. "I tend to get a lot of cuts and scratches." Keeley felt blatantly exposed as he looked down at her bare feet and asked, "Would you like me to—"

"No!" she said, too sharply. She forced a softness into her voice. "Thank you, but I can manage."

Nodding, he gave her the medicine. "So what now?"

She shrugged. "I wait, I guess." *And hope that when Troy gets back, he'll be reasonable enough to let me have my things without making a scene.* "I never thought I'd see the day that I wished I knew how to pick a lock."

"Would you pick it if you could?"

She eyed him suspiciously. "Don't you dare tell me you know how to pick a hotel lock."

"I probably could if I set my mind to it," he said. "But I was speaking rhetorically."

"Rhetorically speaking, yes. If I could, I would," Keeley admitted. "I was hoping to get in and out before Troy got back, to avoid a confrontation." She could almost see the wheels clicking and turning in Digby's mind as a scowl of concentration lined his forehead. Hoping to ward off trouble, she said, "But that doesn't mean I want an accomplice in breaking and entering."

"There are lots of ways to get into a hotel room," he said. "Breaking and entering would be the least desirable of the lot."

"Not to mention that it could get a person arrested."

"You're registered in the room, aren't you?"

She nodded.

"Then you have every right to be there."

"I doubt if the cops would see it that way. The way my luck's running, I'd probably end up getting carted off to jail wearing nothing but your shirt." *And they'd probably put me in a holding cell with you.*

"Not if someone from the hotel opened the door."

"You heard the desk clerk."

"Forget the desk clerk!" Digby said. "They just stand behind the desk and look at computer screens. Housekeeping is in and out of rooms all day and night."

"The room was probably made up hours ago. The maid was in the room next door when we left for brunch."

"But what if you needed something? An ironing board?"

"Wouldn't they be suspicious if I wasn't in the room?" She looked down at herself. "Especially dressed like this."

He stared at her analytically. "Not...necessarily. Is the ice bucket in your room empty?"

"Yes, but—"

"Grab it. Your room key, too. They all look alike. And come with me."

"I can't go anywhere like this."

He looped his large hands around her upper arms. "You're not going *with me*. You've been to the pool, and you're going to get ice."

"I've been to the pool?"

"Where else would you go dressed like that? And I, Troy...what's my last name?"

"Mitchell."

"Troy Mitchell from room—"

"Four-twelve."

"Four-twelve, am going to call from the pool to order an ironing board and iron."

"DO YOU REALLY THINK this is going to work?" Keeley asked as they stole down the stairs to the fourth floor.

"It does in the movies."

"That's hardly reassuring," she said. "Everything works in the movies."

Luckily, no one was around while they reconnoitered the fourth floor, pinpointing the location of the ice machine, elevator and Troy's room.

"Excellent," Digby said, peeping into the hallway from inside the ice room. "You can see the room from here. You'll be able to see whoever brings the board when they knock on the door." He touched her cheek with his forefinger. "It's going to take me at least five minutes to get to the pool, and another five to get back. You know what to do if the ironing board gets here before I do?"

Keeley nodded.

"Good. Now, just relax."

"Easy for you to say," she grumbled. "You're wearing underwear."

An odd, guttural sound rose from Digby's throat. "You could have gone all day without saying that."

"Well, it's true."

"Well, it's not something I need to think about. It's hard enough just knowing that's my shirt sliding off your shoulder."

"You picked a hell of a time to have a testosterone rush."

He laughed wryly. "We don't pick our moments, sweetmeats."

"Just go make the phone call."

He gave a quick bow. "Your wish is my command."

Without a watch, she had no concept of time, but she was sure more than ten minutes had passed by the time he returned.

"No sign of housekeeping yet?" he asked.

She shook her head.

"Anybody come for ice?"

"Just a kid. A boy about nine or ten. He was too intrigued with working the ice dispenser to worry about a half-dressed, nutty lady lurking."

"You're not lurking, you're loitering. Lurking indicates evil intent."

"Thank you Mr. Webster."

"My mother was an English teacher."

"You had a mother?" She said it without thinking.

He scowled. "Yes. I had a mother. I wasn't spawned fully grown."

"It's just hard to imagine you being...little."

"If you ever meet my mother, I'm sure she'd be delighted to fill you in on every embarrassing detail of my infancy." His demeanor changed abruptly, his body tensed. "Fill the bucket," he ordered. "The ironing board just got off the elevator."

She filled the bucket, then peeped down the hall. The uniformed maid was knocking at the door to Troy's room. She stood there a brief eternity before reaching for her passkey.

"Now!" Digby said, squeezing her elbow. "All you have to do is walk in like you have a right to be in that room. Which you do."

"We can only hope the jury sees it the same way," Keeley said as she walked past Digby into the hall, and then sped up in order to catch the door open before the maid left.

4

"It was so easy!" Keeley said, her eyes glowing with excitement as she moved clothes from a drawer into a suitcase. "It's almost scary how easy it was."

"If the party business goes belly up, you always have a career in burglary to fall back on," Digby said.

She stopped her packing long enough to cast a scowl in his direction before turning her attention to the clothes hanging in the closet. The intrigue of finagling her way into the room had wrought a dramatic change in her, and Digby thought that the vibrant young woman he was seeing now was closer to the real Keeley Owens than the vulnerable, wounded bird he'd found stranded in the desert.

She walked back to the suitcase, carrying a bright red dress that Digby could far too easily imagine clinging to her curves. He whistled under his breath. "Speaking of parties—looks like you were planning on stepping out."

"We had tickets to a show tomorrow night." Although she had carefully folded the dress in half before laying it atop the stack of clothes already in the suitcase, she vented her frustration by cramming, rather than gently tucking, the edges down into the case. "Obviously, I won't be wearing it on this trip."

She slammed the case closed and latched it. "I just have to grab my makeup case," she said, shortly before disappearing into the bathroom. Seconds later, a pair of men's briefs, followed closely by a pair of dirty athletic socks, came flying through the door. "Slob can't even pick up after himself!"

The telltale slamming and clanking of items being tossed haphazardly into a bag and the rasp of a heavy zipper told Digby she was packing hastily. She reappeared soon thereafter, carrying a tapestry bag. Her exhilaration was gone, replaced by confused emotions. "Let's get out of here."

Digby picked up the suitcase and took several steps toward the door. But despite Keeley's declared determination to leave, she seemed decidedly unanxious to move. Digby touched her elbow and hated the vulnerability haunting her eyes as she looked up at him. "Are you okay?"

She gave a quick nod and turned with obvious resolve to put the room and all it symbolized behind her. But as she took her first step to leave, voices drifted in from the hall, and there was a click as a card key was slipped into the lock.

The door burst open and a man stumbled in drunkenly. He would have fallen flat on his face if he hadn't been propped up by a young woman who wouldn't have passed a sobriety test in her own right. As he caught himself by clinging to her, the young man released a string of curses.

So this is the boyfriend, Digby thought as he heard Keeley's involuntary gasp. The scene was offensive enough to him; he could only imagine how Keeley must be feeling. The jilted groom's face was flushed from the liquor and his dark hair was badly mussed. He still wore a coat, but his shirt was open halfway to his waist and the woman on which he was leaning was wearing his black bow tie as a choker above the plunging neckline of her blouse.

The boyfriend's reactions were sluggish because of the booze. It took well over a second for him to follow the sound of Keeley's gasp and another couple of seconds for him to study her face before it registered that she was there in front of him. His eyes narrowed. His speech was slurred and his tone was mean. "What the hell are you still doing here?"

Keeley tensed. "Hello, Troy."

"Get the hell out of my room!"

"*Our* room."

Troy snorted derisively. "Not anymore. Not after you walked out on me the way you did." He leaned forward unsteadily. "What the hell are you wearing?"

Though she'd winced involuntarily at the harsh way he'd spoken to her, Keeley ignored the question about the shirt. "I just came to get my things," she said evenly, leading Digby to speculate that she might have prior experience dealing with him in an inebriated state. "I've already found another room."

But Troy was past even the most practiced diplomacy. "That isn't *my* shirt."

Instinctively, Digby moved closer to Keeley and curled his hand around her waist protectively. His movement attracted Troy's attention.

"Who are you?" he roared.

"For starters," Digby replied evenly, "I'm the owner of that shirt."

Troy turned an ugly grimace on Keeley and snorted an unpleasant laugh. "You didn't waste any time, did you?"

Keeley jutted her chin. "You're drunk, Troy."

"I'm not too drunk to see what's going on, you two-timing—" He called her an ugly name, linking it to an offensive adjective. Shrinking away from the hurtful insults, Keeley pressed closer to Digby. Not, Digby knew, out of particular affection for him, but out of desperation for someone to lean on.

"Troy, please," she begged. "Don't say something now you're going to regret—"

"I bet you're not even wearing underwear," Troy said, making a clumsy grab for the bottom edge of the shirt.

Digby couldn't be sure whether he was trying to rip it off her or pull it up to embarrass Keeley. He just knew that he didn't want this drunken idiot touching the shirt or, more to the point, the woman wearing it. And he wasn't about to let it happen. With lightning reflexes, he reached out and grabbed Troy's wrist. "You don't want to *do* anything you'll regret later, now, do you?"

All his life, Digby had been larger than the people around him. With the guidance of his parents, he'd learned never to abuse his size.

With the guidance of his high-school football coach, he'd learned to combine size with attitude to create an atmosphere of intimidation that made violence unnecessary.

He adopted that attitude as Troy's gaze shifted up to his, and he watched the other man slowly evaluate the situation before jerking his wrist away. Digby let go at the first tug of resistance, and the momentum sent Troy stumbling back a step. Righting himself, he squared his shoulders, set his jaw and scowled for a moment at

Digby, then Keeley, and back at Digby. Finally, he dismissed them with a shrug and sniff of disdain. "Who gives a—" he used another strong expletive "—damn?"

As if remembering the presence of the woman with whom he'd entered the room, Troy turned his head until he located her. He draped his arm across her shoulders and gave her a hug, then gave Keeley a hateful look. "It's about time I found myself a real woman anyway."

Digby seldom got angry at any woman, but the smug, gloating expression on the blonde's face at that moment made him want to squash a grapefruit into it.

Keeley swallowed. "Troy—"

Troy's gaze met hers and a tense silence ensued. Digby thought if she begged the jerk to forgive and forget, he might toss his cookies right there in the hotel room.

She swallowed again. "I don't deserve this, Troy."

A muscle twitched in Troy's cheek before he growled, "Just get the hell out of my sight."

"Gladly!" Keeley tipped her head at Digby and started for the door. Digby picked up the suitcase and followed.

"Hey! That's my suitcase!" Troy said.

Keeley stopped and turned to face him. "No, Troy. It's *my* suitcase. It's larger than yours, so we brought it instead of bringing two, remember?"

"What am I supposed to put my clothes in?"

"Gee, Troy," Keeley said, "I don't know. Maybe Suzzi has some room in her bags. After all, a real woman is always prepared." She smiled sweetly. "Just like a Boy Scout."

"You're turning into a real witch, you know that?" Troy said.

Keeley squared her shoulders and shot a glance at Digby before training a sharp look on Troy. "It's a side effect of being treated like a half-eaten Twinkie from yesterday's lunch box."

With that, she yanked the door open and disappeared into the hall. Digby followed. She was moving so fast Digby had to adjust his stride to keep up with her as she scurried toward the stairway. Digby seldom had to adjust his stride to keep up with anyone, especially a short woman with a hurt ankle.

"Great exit line," he said.

"You ought to like it," she said. "You wrote it."

It was obvious to Digby that she was not elated by her impressive exit. He'd never seen a woman her size carrying any form of baggage scale stairs as fast as she climbed the two flights to the sixth floor. She stopped on the landing, shaking and breathing raggedly.

She stood with her back to him, looking tiny with the neck of his shirt hanging off one narrow shoulder. Digby would have had to have been an insensitive oaf not to be aware of the tension in her. *And why not—she'd been dragged through hell and humiliation in a few hours' time.*

He wasn't going anywhere without her, and she showed no intention of leaving—maybe because the stairwell seemed so cut off from the rest of the world.

"How could he think I'd go to bed with a strange man, just like that?" She snapped her fingers in the air. "How could he know me as long as he's known me and believe that of me?"

"You said it yourself—he's hurt."

"That's no excuse!"

Digby shrugged. "I'm glad you realize that."

Her breath caught, then she said, with a defiance at odds with the fatalism in her voice, "I'm not going to cry."

Digby didn't respond to that. Part of him hoped she wouldn't break down. He felt helpless when women cried. Always had. But he wasn't a man who could stand on the rim of a smoking, churning volcano and deny that it's likely to erupt, and if he'd ever seen a woman figuratively smoke and churn, Keeley Owens was that woman.

"He isn't worth it," she said tremulously. "He didn't care—"

"You cared," Digby said. "That's worth a few tears."

The sound that came forth as she turned to face him was the opposite of laughter, a feral cry of despair from deep inside her. Digby moved swiftly, embracing her as the sound swelled into a sob, hugging her as the sob erupted into the inevitable flood. From what he'd just observed, she was entitled to a good, cleansing cry, but he couldn't help feeling also that she was damned lucky to be rid of pretty-boy Troy.

"He was so...hateful!" she said, snuffling. "How could he treat me like that?"

"The man I saw wouldn't know what to do with a decent woman if she came packaged with detailed instructions," Digby said. He, on the other hand, would know just what to do with the woman in his arms. And he planned to show her how a real man treated a woman, now that the boyfriend was out of the picture—beginning with stroking her back and murmuring words of comfort as she emptied her heart and about a gallon of salt water on his chest.

He'd been speculating about what it would be like to hold her since the first moment he'd seen her. He wasn't disappointed. She felt the way a woman should, all soft curves and gentle slopes. He pressed his cheek against her hair and ran his thumb over the velvety skin on her shoulder, breathing in the clean, fresh smell of her and dreaming about other expanses of soft, smooth woman's skin.

"I was so...b-blind," she said. "I thought—" A shudder rocked the full length of her body. She got very still for a moment, then she lifted her head and wiped her right eye with the side of her forefinger.

Digby swept his thumb under her left eye, smearing the remnants of a tear over her cheek. "Better?"

She gave a tight little nod. Spying the wet splotch on the front of his shirt, she frowned endearingly and touched it with her fingertips. "I'm...sorry."

He captured her hand, covered it, curled his fingers around it. "It'll dry."

"At least I wasn't wearing mascara." Her chin quivered, and for an instant, he feared she might burst into a fresh onslaught of tears. Instead, she wheezed, "What if I'd married him?"

She was coming out of shock, reacting to what might have been with the same quaking realization of someone who'd felt a bullet whiz past her ear. He'd never seen anyone look as lost or helpless. He'd never wanted as desperately to comfort anyone, to make everything all right. His hands went to her face to cradle it. He poised his mouth to speak and searched for words of reassurance, but instead of speaking, he lowered his face and touched his lips to hers tentatively. When she didn't draw back, he combed his fingers into her hair, molding her scalp, and claimed her mouth in earnest, tasting salt and a trace of white wine and the promise of paradise on her lips.

Keeley slid her arms around his waist, clinging to him. He was so firm, so solid. She leaned into his superior strength, savoring the hardness of his body next to hers. It was glorious to surrender herself to sensations, knowing she was capable of passion after the ugly scene with Troy, which had left her feeling hollow and emotionally depleted.

The kiss ended as naturally as it had begun. Keeley let her arms fall slowly to her sides as Digby lifted his head and looked down at her face. They were still close enough for her to feel his physical response to their bodies touching. He traced her exposed collarbone with his forefinger as though he found it fascinating and beautiful.

His exhaled breath skittered hotly over her sensitized skin, and she was struck, as she shivered in reaction, by the impropriety of their situation. Not only had she been running around a hotel half-dressed, she'd just shared a passionate kiss with a stranger in a public place.

She inhaled sharply and tensed. Digby pulled his hand away. "I wasn't planning on taking advantage of you."

"No one said you were," Keeley said, ducking her head to dodge his gaze. *At least not in words.*

Curling his finger under her chin, he urged her face up until she was forced to look at him. "You just looked like you needed someone to—" Words failed him.

"Kiss it and make it better?" she asked, taking a stab at humor.

"Something like that."

She closed her eyes and sighed dismally. "How many good deeds do you have to do to get that merit badge you're working on?"

"You were as close to me as prepasted wallpaper," he said. "You're bound to know there was more to it than pity."

"That's not—" She stopped midsentence and turned her back to him. "I can't think right now. I just want to go to my room and—" *Brush my teeth. Play solitaire. Watch something old and stupid on television. Curl into a tight little ball and disappear.* Put on underwear.

"Keeley, Keeley, Keeley!" He shook his head with mock impatience. "The last thing you need is to hole up in a strange hotel room all alone sulking."

She looked over her shoulder at him. "And I guess you can tell me just what I *do* need."

"It doesn't take a Ph.D. in psychology to figure it out. You need to be around people."

"I'm not in the mood."

"That, my dear Miss Owens, is exactly *why* you need to go out and have some fun." He teased his fingertip along her bare shoulder. She twitched the way she might if a fly had landed there. Undaunted, he blew on the nape of her neck, ruffling her hair and sending a tremor of titillation down her spine. "Come on, Keeley. You're in Las Vegas. Put on your red dress and let's go out and have some fun."

"Together?"

"Yes. Together." He sounded vaguely amused, but there was a sensual note in his voice that made Keeley wary.

"I don't think so," she said.

He bent to pick up her suitcase and then cupped her elbow with his free hand. "You don't have to decide right this minute."

He walked her to her room and slid the suitcase onto the luggage stand. They looked at each other awkwardly.

"Thanks—" She hesitated before finishing lamely, "For everything."

He nodded. His gaze lingered on her face. "I wish you'd change your mind about going out tonight. I would enjoy the company."

"In the mood I'm in, I'd be about as much company as a piece of lint."

His face softened appealingly as he chuckled softly. "I used to play with lint when I was a kid."

"You must have been a weird kid."

"I was always curious about things."

"About lint?" she asked dubiously.

"It was fuzzy," he said. His gaze settled hotly on her face, warming it. "I had to find out what it felt like— what happened when I touched it."

He was talking about *lint!* for Pete's sake. It just didn't *seem* like that was what he was talking about. Keeley swallowed. "Oh."

After a spell of silence, he said, "I'm going to knock on your door in two hours—in case you change your mind."

He dropped a quick kiss on her cheek before leaving through the door that connected their rooms. Just be-

fore closing the door on his side, he poked his head
back into her room and grinned. "Be sure to lock your
side. You don't want the bogeyman to get you."

Keeley frowned as the bolt on his side engaged with
a *thlunk* and then his words came through the closed
door as clear as a radio broadcast. "I sure would like to
see you in that red dress!"

Speaking of the bogeyman! Not only had he managed
to make her feel silly about wanting the door locked,
he'd put her in a position of feeling guilty if she didn't
go out with him. She dug a pair of panties from her
suitcase and stepped into them, then carried her
makeup tote into the bathroom. After taking two aspirin, as much for her throbbing head as for her injured
ankle, she arranged the things she needed for her daily
routine within easy reach on the vanity. Facial cleanser,
toothbrush and paste, hairbrush, gel, spray, the zipper
bag with her makeup in it—she could have replaced
the entire lot of them in a single stroll through a discount store but, somehow, because she'd used each of
them under more normal circumstances, they seemed
almost a part of her. Just having them there, within
reach, reassured her, probably because she'd been cut
off from them earlier.

She scrubbed her face, slathered on moisturizer, then
saturated a washcloth with cool water, wrung it out
and stretched out on the bed with the cold compress
over her eyes. If the giant in the next room thought she
was going anywhere, she thought drowsily, he was in
for a close encounter with reality. After the day she'd
had, she had every intention and, as far as she was concerned, an inalienable right, to hole up in her room and

work through her misery any way she chose to deal with it.

Gradually, she dozed off. When she awoke, the aspirin had kicked in. Her head had cleared and she felt rested—so rested that she was surprised to discover that she'd actually slept less than an hour. With her headache gone, she decided to start that book she'd been wanting to read, but when she opened her suitcase to get the book, the red dress captured her attention and drove sharp shards of memory through her heart. She'd been so excited when she packed for this trip.

Except for a high-school trip to Washington, D.C., the only traveling she'd ever done had been to destinations within Florida. This was to have been her first real just-for-fun, out-of-state vacation. Troy had been looking forward to gambling and drinking and partying until dawn; Keeley's head had been spinning at the prospect of seeing a show featuring famous performers, alive and in person.

Lifting the dress from the suitcase, she walked to the mirror and held it up in front of her. The brilliant color brought out a natural blush in her cheeks, and the silky fabric draped elegantly as she held it up. The dress was one of her favorites. Wearing it, she felt sexy and pretty and female. And now, she'd made it all the way to Las Vegas, and she wasn't going to get to wear it.

Hugging the dress to her, she sank onto the edge of the bed. If only Troy hadn't won that stupid jackpot! If he'd just gambled away their money without winning anything, they wouldn't have gone out celebrating. Brian wouldn't have jokingly suggested that Troy marry her, and Cork wouldn't have laughed, goading

Troy, as much as daring him, to marry her. They would never have gone to that chapel. They'd still be having fun—

Troy would still be having fun, she thought. *She* would still be watching Troy have fun and pretending that she was enjoying the trip as much as he was. He would be drinking too much, she would be pretending she wasn't noticing how much he was drinking.

Her relationship with Troy had been implanted with a ticking time bomb. Sooner or later it was going to end. The unexpected detour to the chapel had just brought about the inevitable sooner rather than later.

Keeley ran her hand over the slick, red cloth folded in her lap absently, the way she might stroke a small animal. A glitzy show with celebrity performers was a small consideration compared to a decision that would affect the rest of her life but, damn it, she hated the thought of making it all the way to Vegas and having nothing but unpleasant memories. She'd seen a casino, lounge and a tacky wedding chapel and she'd ended a relationship she'd thought would last forever, but she had yet to get even a glimpse at the glitter for which the city was famous.

Troy and the others would go to the show tomorrow night without her. She was the one who'd really wanted to see it, and now she was being cut out of the fun. Troy wasn't downstairs pining away in the room they'd shared. He was either down there with Suzzi consoling him or out partying.

It didn't seem fair.

It *wasn't* fair.

But it didn't *have* to be this way. All she had to do was put on her dress and be ready to go when Digby knocked on the door.

5

DIGBY PAUSED in the hallway, silently speculating on the odds that Keeley would answer his knock. He guessed the chances were at least sixty-forty in his favor that she would. He'd seen her vulnerability, but he'd also witnessed her resilience. Busted relationship or not, she didn't strike him as the type who'd sit around sulking when she had any choice in the matter, especially when Pretty Boy was downstairs with a blonde.

He knocked heavily, three times in rapid succession, then listened for signs of movement on the other side of the door. Muffled footsteps alerted him to her approach, then he heard the sliding of the chain lock. The door opened and Keeley, resplendent in red, greeted him with a tentative smile. Digby's breath caught in his throat.

He couldn't pinpoint what it was that made the dress so spectacular on her. It was not revealing, certainly not as revealing as the wedding dress. Or his shirt, for that matter. The neckline was modest, the knee-length hemline chaste. But there was something about the way the soft, red cloth slid over the curves of her body like a caress that made a man want to do the same thing. At least Digby did.

Suspecting that she knew exactly what he was thinking, he self-consciously returned her smile and held out the clear plastic florist's box, taking pleasure in the surprised delight that registered on her face as she studied the white orchid inside.

"A corsage," she said with an edge of disbelief. Her fingers trembled a little as she opened the box so she could admire the flowers without the distortion of the plastic. "I haven't had a corsage since my high-school prom. And I've never had orchids."

"You're overdue, then."

She tilted her head back to look at his face. "But you didn't know whether I would be going with you or not. I didn't even know."

"It's Vegas," he said. "I gambled. Besides, it's not a prize for going out with me. I would have given it to you regardless. I wanted to surprise you. After everything that's happened today, you deserved something...pretty."

Careful to keep the box upright in her hand, she threw her arms around his neck, raised on tiptoe and brushed his cheek with a kiss. "Thank you."

There was nothing sexual in the spontaneous demonstration of appreciation. There was nothing specifically sexual in Digby's response, either, but there was a great deal of pleasure. Chuckling, he replied, "You're welcome."

He was beginning to like Keeley Owens.

A lot.

She drew away from him slowly, but he wasn't ready to let her go. Capping her shoulders with his hands, he told her, "But, for the record, I'm glad you're coming. It wouldn't be much fun going to a show alone."

"We're going to a Las Vegas show?"

She sounded like a kid who'd been told she was going to the circus. Digby grinned. "You're easily awed."

"I grew up in a small town," she said. "I'm still getting used to movie theaters with more than one
screen." She gingerly lifted the corsage from the box,
handling it as though it would crumble to ash if she
jarred it.

"Here," Digby said, taking it from her. "Let me."
Hoping to put her at ease, he grinned affably and
pulled the long, pearl-headed pin from the ribbon at
the base of the corsage. Holding the flower in front of
her shoulder, he tilted slightly to the left and then to
the right, eyeing it the way an artist would a masterpiece in progress before actually pressing it against her
dress with his left hand and positioning the pin between the thumb and forefinger of his right hand.
"There's an art to this."

There was a strange intimacy in having the knuckles
of his huge hand pressed firmly into her shoulder as he
expertly lifted her dress a fraction of an inch away
from her skin and held it there while he fastened the
orchid with impressive expertise. While his move-
ments were efficient, the warm pressure of his touch
seemed anything but clinical, and Keeley found his
closeness disconcerting. "You, uh, must have done this
before," she said.

He smiled slyly. "It's half the fun of buying a woman
a corsage."

"What's the other half?" she asked as Digby stepped
back to admire his handiwork a second or two.

His gaze settled on Keeley's face. "Getting hugged,
of course."

That she didn't doubt. Women probably lined up

and took a number for the chance to hug him. And more.

"Ready?" he asked, offering her an elbow. Nodding, she looped her arm through his.

"The theater is in a hotel about three blocks from here," he said as they left the hotel. "How's the ankle?"

"The tape really helps," she said. "I can make three blocks."

"If it starts hurting, just let me know."

"And you'll carry me piggyback?" she teased.

"I was going to say we'd take a cab," he said, tilting his head toward a taxi stand on the corner, "but if you insist—"

Donning what Keeley was beginning to think of as his "mischievous-boy" expression, he dipped one knee as if to kneel.

"Digby!" Keeley said, tugging at his arm as though she could keep him from doing so.

He straightened and shrugged. "Just trying to oblige."

The theater was set up amphitheater style, with three semicircular tiers surrounding the stage. The front row of each tier was made up of tiny round tables for two, the adjacent rows narrow rectangular tables that seated four on each side. Their seats were at one of the cozy little tables on the front row of the second tier. While Digby ordered a carafe of wine from the cocktail waitress making the rounds, Keeley perused the program, determinedly searching the cast list and performer bios for familiar names or faces.

Digby could feel months of tension slowly melting away as he watched her. Her enthusiasm, so genuine and refreshing, was exactly what he'd needed to remind him that there was still a world beyond the walls of his workshop. He'd been sequestered in that room, surrounded by nuts and bolts and charts and notes for months, as obsessed with the assembler he was building as Dr. Frankenstein with his monster.

"I've heard of this guy!" she said excitedly. "You remember him, don't you? He used to play the father on *The McMitchells*."

He vaguely recalled the old sitcom from his teenage years. He leaned toward Keeley to look at her program. "Good grief! Let me see that picture. How old is that guy now?" He was less interested in the picture than the opportunity to get closer to Keeley.

"'This veteran performer reprises a classic vaudeville act with a contemporary slant,'" she read aloud, then resumed skimming. "Oh my gosh!"

"What?" Digby said, leaning again. "Who?"

"Chet Blane. He used to be the lead singer for the Grumps. They made 'Until I Hear Your Voice.' It was my favorite song my entire freshman year in high school. My best friends and I wrote to his fan club for photos and hung his picture above our beds." Her gaze met his. "I can't believe I'm really going to see Chet Blane in person."

"You're not going to scream and swoon or throw underwear, are you?"

"No!" Keeley said, laughing. "I'll just sit here and drool quietly."

Digby stretched his arm across the back of her chair. "Drool as loudly as you like. You don't get a chance to see your teen idol every day."

"Not even every year," she said. Her expression

turned serious. "If you hadn't—" She paused and took a breath.

He dipped his head to kiss her briefly. "I'm glad you decided to come along. It would have been a drag without you."

"Digby—" There were so many things she could have said, should have said. But his name was all that slipped out, and as his head lowered to hers again, her mind filled with the reasons this couldn't, shouldn't, be happening. *She hardly knew this man. Just hours ago, she'd been two words away from marrying another man, a man with whom she'd been living for over a year.*

But as adamantly as she told herself this couldn't be happening, shouldn't be happening, it *was* happening. As though they'd set off some invisible switch, the houselights dimmed as his face drew nearer. There was no embrace, no groping, no touching at all except for his mouth pressing against her lips, claiming them; his tongue teasing over them. And yet—it was enough. Enough to make her heart beat faster, to steal her breath away, to preempt her conscious awareness of anything other than the heat and texture of his lips. And then, just as their mouths broke contact, a cymbal crash rose from the orchestra pit, signaling the impending rise of the curtain. It, and the brass fanfare that followed, seemed more like proverbial fireworks sparked by their kiss.

Their gazes locked and held for several seconds before Digby said, "The show's starting." He smiled gently. "You wouldn't want to miss Chet."

The curtain lifted to reveal a jagged-edged pyramid that looked like a massive free-form sculpture. As the stage lights went up, the pyramid evolved into a chorus of nine women wearing floor-length capes and plumed headgear that jutted two feet above their heads. Slowly, moving with the regal grace of old-world monarchs, they descended a spiral staircase and lined up on the stage. Spreading their arms, they moved in unison to the music, their silver lamé capes shimmering and fluttering like gossamer wings, changing color under the filtered spotlights.

Spellbound, Keeley sat back to enjoy the performance. She didn't try to make sense of the fact that it seemed perfectly natural for her to be here with Digby, perfectly natural for Digby's arm to be across the back of her chair, perfectly right for her to rest her neck against his thick forearm while she drank in the ambience.

The opening number ended with the chorus girls with their backs to the audience, arms fully extended toward the sky. The stage lights faded, then came up again. Suddenly the capes flew upward, disappearing into the darkness above the stage like predatory birds into the night, and the orchestra broke into a rock song with a manic beat. The two-piece costumes the chorus girls were wearing were skimpier than any bikini Keeley had ever seen parading up and down Daytona Beach, the tops a thin string across their backs, the thong bottoms hiding very little as the dancers gyrated their exercise-hardened buns to the beat of the music.

Abruptly, they spun to face the audience, strutting to the front edge of the stage. The tops of the costumes framed their breasts, supporting and pushing them up like underwires without covering them. Keeley gasped. "They're topless!"

"Yes," Digby whispered. "I noticed." His arm

curved around her shoulders for a quick hug and his lusty chuckle vibrated into her ear. "You're in Vegas, baby."

"Yes." She giggled delightedly. "I'm in Vegas."

The chorus danced themselves into two lines flanking the base of the stairs, and the music faded to a percussive hum before segueing into "Until I Hear Your Voice." Spotlights crisscrossed the darkened stage and merged at the top of the stairs, and an amplified disembodied voice boomed, "Ladies and gentleman, we are pleased to present the vocalist who made this song number one on the charts for eight consecutive weeks. Please welcome Mr....Chet...Blane!"

The singer was older and rounder, but in his tight jeans, black knee boots and white silk shirt with big sleeves, wide collar and a V neck that plunged almost to his waist, he might have stepped from Keeley's adolescent fantasies. Keeley applauded enthusiastically and told Digby, "Connie and Tracy aren't going to believe me when I tell them about this."

Digby laughed and hugged her again, although he wasn't certain she even noticed. He couldn't remember the last time he'd been around a woman so spontaneous and unaffected. Her enthusiasm was the perfect antidote for the stress that had driven him to take a vacation. *Keeley* herself was the best medicine for his sagging morale. Less than eight hours after first laying eyes on her, his workshop and the unfinished assembler seemed as remote as a distant planet.

Thinking that this was going to be a memorable vacation, he sat back to enjoy the show. And enjoy Keeley enjoying it. She was so engrossed in the glitzy performance that she never noticed he was watching her as avidly as he watched the performers.

The vaudeville routine featuring the veteran sitcom star was near the end of the program. It was a variation of the old lifesize-doll sketch, which opened with the actor scratching his head as he examined a cardboard box covered with Fragile, Handle with Care and This Side Up labels. Discovering a label that said, Pull Tab To Open, he pulled the tab, and the box opened to reveal a lifesize doll inside. The actress playing the doll was wearing a bikini bottom and a pair of tasseled pasties.

"They don't believe in clothes in this town, do they?" Keeley whispered.

"That must be what they meant by a contemporary slant," Digby replied.

The actor found an enormous, oversize remote control and tentatively pushed a button. Moving in jerky, mechanical motions, accompanied by comical sounds from the percussion section of the orchestra, the doll raised her arm.

The actor pushed the button again and she lowered it. Finally, after finding the buttons that controlled eyebrow quirks and high kicks, he located the button that made her step free of the box.

He continued experimenting in a hammy performance, finding buttons that made her pucker her lips and hitch her hips from side to side. Each choppy motion was underscored by an appropriate rimshot, click, whirl or whistle.

The audience response grew warmer and rowdier with each of the sexy maneuvers. But when the twist of a knob on the control panel resulted in the "doll" flexing her right breast in a motion that made the tassel on her pastie swing, there was a veritable explosion of ribald laughter throughout the theater at the actor's wide-eyed, slack-jaw surprise.

Riding the raucous applause, he tried the knob next to the one he'd just turned and her left breast twitched. With a dumb grin, he began playing with the knobs, alternating them while the tassels spun in circles—one at a time, simultaneously in the same direction, simultaneously in opposite directions. That physical feat combined with the actress's blank, baby-doll expression and the actor's hilarious double takes drew deafening applause and hysterical guffaws from the audience, so she continued to spin the tassels in opposite directions.

Keeley looked at Digby, her face a study of surprise, bemusement, embarrassment and disbelief. "That *can't* be possible."

"Extraordinary muscular coordination," Digby agreed with a grin. Her reaction was infinitely more entertaining than the high jinks onstage.

Her gaze went back to the spinning pasties, and she shook her head in consternation. "Two directions at once."

Digby suddenly sat bolt upright. "Dual, independently operating swivel joints. Of course!" It was so simple. How could he have missed it?

"Digby?" Concern marked Keeley's face.

Laughing aloud, he drew her into a bear hug. "I knew you were going to be good for me the moment I saw you dancing in the street!"

"IS YOUR ANKLE bothering you?" Digby asked.

"It got a little stiff when we were sitting," Keeley

said. She'd been trying to hide the fact that it was hurting, but she must have been involuntarily favoring it.

Digby stretched his arms across her shoulders. "Lean on me. Take some of the pressure off."

"It's not that bad," she said. "We're just a block from the hotel."

"If you don't lean on me, I'll have to sling you over my shoulders like a sack of potatoes," Digby said.

Keeley's eyes narrowed. "You'd do that, wouldn't you?"

"Yes. And you'd feel pretty silly with that cute little bottom of yours in the air. Now, put your arm around my waist and lean!"

With a shrug of acquiescence, she complied.

"Better, isn't it?" he said.

"Yes," she admitted grudgingly. "Much." It was better than better. It was damned good. To have someone taking care of her. To have someone holding her. To have someone to hold on to. Not just because of her ankle, but because of her wounded pride and ravaged self-esteem.

Much too good. Much too tempting.

"If I saw this in a movie, I'd think it was corny and contrived," she said, trying to lighten the mood a little.

"In a movie, you'd be *pretending* your ankle hurt," he said.

"And I'd forget which ankle was supposed to be twisted and you'd find out I was faking it, just to get close to you."

He stopped and looked down at her, touching her face with his fingertips. "You don't have to go to that kind of trouble to get close to me, Keeley. Where you're concerned, I'm easy. I want you as close to me as I can get you."

"Digby—" She'd hoped to forestall a kiss, but the name came out as a sigh of encouragement that he scarcely needed. Even as her tongue touched the tip of her palate to form the word, his lips moved inexorably closer to hers.

"We shouldn't be doing this," she managed to say.

He stopped just short of touching his mouth to hers. "I'm a man, you're a woman, and in case you haven't noticed, we set off sparks every time we get within ten feet of each other. Where's the problem?"

"I can't think straight," she said.

"That, Miss Owens, is the best news I've heard tonight." He kissed her then. Solidly. Thoroughly. Passionately.

She forgot the reasons she should be resisting him. Lost in the moment, she forgot about yesterday, today and tomorrow. In the magic of the kiss, she forgot everything except the way he made her feel when he touched her—alive and desirable and passionate.

When Digby tore his mouth away from hers abruptly, she could only look up into his eyes, trying to focus as she silently demanded to know why. And then she heard the clapping, the horrible explosions of sound that managed to convey disdain and sarcasm in their hatefully slow pace, and her gaze followed Digby's to the man producing that abhorrent sound.

"Troy!" she blurted. Humiliation burned its way up from her chest to her cheeks. The whole gang was with him: Suzzi, hanging on his arm; Brian and his girlfriend; Cork and a young woman Keeley didn't recognize.

"You remembered my name," Troy said sarcastically. "I'm touched." The meanness of his attack, as much as the slurring of his words and the brightness in his eyes, told her that he was still drinking. He was sometimes self-centered and often devil-may-care when he was sober, but he wasn't mean unless he'd had too much to drink.

"I'm not going to argue with you, Troy." Nevertheless, she steeled herself for a confrontation.

He glowered at her a long time, and Keeley forced herself to endure the venomous rancor in his eyes. If looks could kill—

"I hope that means you'll have your stuff out of my apartment by the time I get back to Florida," he said.

Sadness pierced her heart as she nodded tersely, not so much for what could have been as for what she'd once believed there would be. She'd been seeing everything through the rose-colored lenses of youth and dream-laced idealism. Now she saw him as he really was, saw herself as she was, saw the same uncrossable chasm between them that she'd seen in the wedding chapel.

"I will," she said softly.

Troy laughed. It was an ugly laugh, filled with pain. "Now you say it."

They stared at each other, for only a few seconds, and then Troy visibly put up a shield of pride to defend himself from the feelings they'd once shared. His jaw squared as he jutted his chin defiantly. Snubbing her, he turned to his friends. "We came to Vegas to have fun. Let's go out and have some."

They closed ranks around him, following without a backward glance as he stalked away. But Troy just couldn't leave without a final word. Stopping abruptly, he turned to glare at Keeley one last time. "If I find anything of yours when I get back, it's going straight into the trash."

Not wanting to provoke him, Keeley nodded mutely. He hesitated. Then, apparently satisfied that he'd made his point, Troy left, leading his pack of friends. Keeley slumped against Digby, grateful to have his solid strength to lean on.

"You live with him?" Digby asked thoughtfully.

"Not anymore," Keeley said. She exhaled a shuddering sigh. "Let's go in."

Though she continued leaning on him for support, Digby sensed Keeley's withdrawal in her sullen silence. His suspicions were confirmed when they reached her room. Glad that they had at least enough luck that the hallway was deserted, he pulled her into a full embrace for a good-night kiss.

The motions were the same, their mouths touched as before, but the heat and closeness of their earlier kiss were missing.

Her reticence did not surprise as much as sadden him. Reluctantly, he cut the kiss short and let his arms slip from around her. "Your ex-boyfriend sure has lousy timing."

"It's not only Troy, or what just happened," she said. "It's...me, too."

"You were doing fine before he showed up." He coaxed her chin up with his fingertips until their gazes locked.

She spoke softly. "This evening was... It was exactly what I needed, and you were...sweet and attentive and—"

His shoulders rose in a shrug of resignation and he released a sigh of pure frustration. "Yeah. I'm a prince of a guy. I get that from all the girls."

She diffused his sarcasm with a sad little smile, then kissed her fingertips and pressed them to his lips.

One side of his mouth lifted in a crooked grin. "Is that the best you can do for a prince?"

Slipping her arms over his shoulders and around his neck, she pressed her mouth to his briefly and hugged him before backing away.

Grinning, he cupped her elbows and pulled her back to him for a more thorough kiss, after which he continued holding her, until the sound of laughter filtered down the hall from the direction of the elevators. Groaning, Digby raised his head. "I hate making out in public. Someone's always interrupting."

"I probably ought to..." Her voice trailed off as she reached into her handbag for her room key.

"I could think of half a dozen ways to finish that sentence for you, and I'll bet not one of them would be the one you were thinking," Digby said.

"Probably not," Keeley said as she inserted the key into the electronic lock. She pulled it out and turned the knob. The door opened with a click.

"If you...get lonely, or need anything, just knock on the wall," Digby said. "I'll be in bed, not sleeping. After I take a cold shower."

She looked at his face as he spoke and, seeing the yearning in his eyes, she experienced a pang of sadness for what might have been under different circumstances.

He leaned for a quick-drop kiss and grinned devilishly. "You'd better make sure that connecting door is locked."

"Good night, Digby," she said firmly, stepping into her room.

Once sequestered in her room, with the privacy and chain locks engaged, she suddenly felt isolated and cut off. The issues she'd been holding at bay descended into the void to taunt her the minute she opened her suitcase for something to sleep in and found a choice between the sleep shirt she'd worn with Troy last night and the silk boxer and camisole set she'd brought along to surprise Troy. She'd hoped that she and Troy could end their relationship graciously and remain friends, but his attitude in their latest confrontation had squelched that hope. Obviously they weren't going to be friends anytime soon, if ever. And on top of all the emotional turmoil, she was going to have to move. Soon. The prospect was overwhelming. First she'd have to find a place, order a phone, start electrical service, fill out change-of-address forms—

None of which she could do tonight, she reminded herself. Tonight she just wanted to get some sleep so she could face the issues fresh when a new day dawned. Unable to bring herself to wear the sleep shirt again after everything that had happened today—she would have to wash and bleach it before she could wear it again—she took the silk boxer set from her suitcase. She'd bought it to sleep in after her big night on the town in Vegas. Well, she'd had a night on the town, and she was going to sleep in it.

Although she'd bathed earlier, she took a quick shower, this time using her own shower gel and after-bath cream, so that her skin felt as soft and smooth as the silk settling over it as she donned the wispy camisole and light-as-air boxers.

The sensual pampering soothed her physically, but emotionally, she was a hopeless mess. She was exhausted, but restless; sad over the way her relationship with Troy had ended, but relieved to have faced the inevitable and put an end to it. She knew she should be missing Troy as she crawled between the sheets of the unfamiliar bed but, oddly, last night and all the previous nights she'd spent with Troy seemed like distant history. The person she thought of as she lay there trying to find the energy to turn out the light was the man in the next room.

Rolling onto her side, she found herself nose to petal with the corsage, which she'd set on the bedside table when she'd taken it off her dress. Her first orchids. She traced a petal with her forefinger as she studied the delicate flowers. They looked like the finest porcelain, but their texture was a blend of velvet and satin.

They were so perfect, so elegant. And yet, exotic, the way the entire evening had been. Orchids, topless dancers, the sex symbol of her teen years and spinning tassels. Las Vegas, flashy and loud; Digby, solid and warm.

A sob lodged in her throat but, refusing to cry, she buried her face in the pillow and groaned. From the heart. From the soul. Then she lay very still, lusting for sleep in the still silence of the night in a strange bed, in a strange place, far away from home.

She was so alone—more alone than she could remember ever having been in her entire life. And as she lay there, chasing the obliviousness of slumber, the thought occurred to her that Troy wasn't alone. She was as sure as any woman could be that he'd been faithful to her when they were together, but she knew him well enough to know that when his ego was wounded, he was not likely to turn down the solace of a woman as prepared to provide it as Suzzi. The others weren't alone, either. Brian was with his girlfriend, and Cork was probably sharing space with the woman who'd been hanging on his arm earlier.

Keeley punched the pillow in frustration. She and Digby were probably the only two people in the city of Las Vegas who were alone. It wasn't fair.

Restlessly she flopped over, trying to get comfortable, and a piercing pain shot up her leg. "Damn!" she muttered. Just her luck she'd twist her ankle after she'd decided it wasn't hurting bad enough for her to need aspirin. Now if she didn't get up and take some, the new pain would keep her awake.

Frowning, she limped to the bathroom and downed two tablets, chasing them with lukewarm tap water. *Damned fine vacation,* she thought. *Damned fine.*

A flash of muted red in the mirror caught her eye as she turned to leave the bathroom. Digby's T-shirt dangled crookedly from the clothes hook on the door. Taking it down, she draped it over her arm and, without thinking, carried it back to bed with her and hugged it as she settled under the covers.

Had it really been just hours ago that he'd loaned it to her?

Had it really been just last night that she'd arrived in Las Vegas with Troy, excited about a real vacation? Just this morning that she'd gotten dressed anticipating a day of fun? Just this afternoon that she'd stood in that wedding chapel and made a decision that changed the rest of her life? Just over an hour ago that she'd been limping home, exhilarated over having seen a real Las Vegas show, feeling cozy and safe as she leaned against Digby for support?

Had she really been alone in this room for only an hour? It seemed like half a lifetime.

She heard something then. A sound from the next room. A shuffle. Movement of some sort. Digby, tossing in his sleep? Digby, not sleeping, as he'd predicted.

The way I'm not sleeping.

Alone.

Lonely.

Frustrated.

The only other person in Las Vegas alone tonight.

She sat up. There must be plenty of good reasons for her to stay right where she was and leave everything the way it was, but she couldn't think of any at the moment. Or, to be more accurate, she didn't *want* to think of them. She didn't want to think at all. She wanted to feel. She wanted to bury her face in a broad chest and have strong arms around her and *feel* to the point of obliviousness.

And not five feet away from her, there was a man who'd made it clear he wanted the same thing.

She got out of bed and went to the connecting door. She reached for it, touched the lock, but didn't turn it.

Fools rush in where angels fear to tread. She could almost hear her grandmother's voice. She leaned her forehead against the door and drew in a deep breath. *Was she really going to do this?*

Lifting her head, she pursed her lips and emptied her lungs. She was no angel tonight. Tonight, she was just a lonely woman who'd rather be a little foolish than be alone.

Her hand covered the knob again and, this time, she twisted until the lock clicked. She would knock ever so softly on his door. If he was sleeping, sleeping the sleep of a man of good deeds and a clear conscience, he probably wouldn't even hear her. If he was awake—

If he was awake, then maybe, just maybe, he was as lonely as she was.

Holding her breath, she pulled the door open, ready to knock on the door that led into his room. But she didn't have to knock.

Because the door on his side was already wide-open.

She took two steps forward and whispered his name.

6

DIGBY WAS SITTING in bed, his shoulders propped against a sea of pillows, listening to earphones hooked to a portable CD player and writing on a tablet braced against his right knee. She must have cast a shadow as she entered, because he seemed to sense her presence and looked up. His features registered surprise, followed closely by a smile. "Keeley."

Setting the earphones and tablet aside, he got up to greet her. He was wearing a pair of faded knit shorts that matched the shirt he'd loaned her. Golden hair lightly furred his long, muscular legs and broad chest. He walked to her, and his eyes slid over her face, heating it with the desire she read in his expression as he looked at her. He touched her hair with a gentleness that defied the hugeness of his hands. "You're beautiful."

"No," she said. "I'm just—" *Passably pretty.* She knew men found her attractive, but conversations didn't stop when she entered a room.

"You unlocked the door," he said, ignoring her denial.

"I—" *Was lonely.* "Digby, I—"

He combed his fingers into her hair. "Did you come to talk?"

"No," she said, sighing as his thumb played with the rim of her ear. She didn't want to talk any more than she wanted to think. Tilting her head back, she met his gaze. "I didn't come to talk."

Smiling sweetly, he wrapped his arm around her waist and pulled her against him. "Thank God."

His mouth took hers in a kiss more daring than their earlier ones. He was claiming her, body and mind; absorbing her; consuming her; telling her in a language more primitive than words that they were moving into a new arena of intimacy. It was exciting, stimulating to explore that new intimacy and test new ways of touching. Her toe brushed the arch of his bare foot. Her shin rubbed against the coarse hair on his calf. His knee dented her thigh. His splayed hand, large and strong, warmed her back through the thin silk camisole.

And it felt good. Good to be with a fellow human being. Good to feel the passion of desire he stirred in her. Good to feel the passion she stirred in him. Good to feel female and desirable and alive.

She forced herself to tear her mouth from his. "Do you have—"

"I'll take care of it," he assured her. His fingers were still woven in her hair, tilting her head back. She closed her eyes and exhaled languidly as he trailed kisses over her cheek and down to her neck.

Digby's words skittered over her moist, sensitized skin as he angled his mouth from her neck and growled, "You even sound delicious."

Keeley pressed closer, as though she could meld with him, disappear into him. They were of the same mind, shared the same needs, burned with the same heat. He held her tighter, kissed her deeply, took his hand from her hair to wrap his arm around her. His body was still unfamiliar to her; his size new to her.

His solid, muscular bulk filled her arms. He surrounded her, swallowing her like a feather comforter, warming her with a fire from within.

When he carried her to the bed, it was like being swept up into a cloud and floating on sensation. He laid her down and sat on the edge of the bed admiring her, consuming her with his eyes before actually touching her. Gently, his fingers brushed her hair from her face and then slid forward, over her ear, down her neck, to her shoulder. He touched the narrow silk tube strap of her camisole and, smiling, slipped his finger beneath the strap and pushed it aside, then traced her shoulder from the top of her arm to the graceful depression at the base of her throat.

His touch was tender, more poignant and erotic because of the strength of his large, powerful hands. He could have crushed her throat closed with little effort, but instead, he touched her with that careful gentleness and reverence.

Cradling his face, she whispered, "Thank you." For rescuing her. For entertaining her. For being there when she needed human companionship. For tenderness and kindness. For passion. For making her feel not only female and desirable, but desired.

He moved his hand to her face and traced her lips tremulously with his thumb. "You don't have to thank me for wanting you," he said. "All I had to do was look at you to do that."

The acuity with which he'd read her thoughts and understood what she was trying to say was almost frightening—but not nearly as frightening as his next words: "This is so much more than that. So... much...more."

She understood what he meant, too. Understood that she had been more than lonely when she passed through the door into his room. He was more than just a convenient male to curl up with, and what was happening between them was more than a one-night vacation fling. The thought that she should protest, deny, flitted through her mind, but she had neither the will nor opportunity as his mouth covered hers again and she became lost in his kiss.

The sense of destiny he'd implied colored their lovemaking. Each touch, while new enough to carry with it an aura of discovery, conveyed also a sense of inevitability as it thrilled. She didn't want to think. She wanted only to feel and enjoy.

And enjoy she did—the expertise of his large hands as they slid over her skin and inside the silk garments she wore. The way his body felt against hers: hard, soft, smooth, downy and male. The way his mouth caressed and teased. The intensity of his lovemaking. His energy. His patience. His impetuousness. His power. His control. His generosity. His hunger for her. His obvious enjoyment of her. The sounds he made when she explored him. Caressed him. Pressed closer to him. The way his breathing got deep and heavy when she strained against him.

He took her gently, filled her completely, stroked her lovingly while they sought a compatible rhythm. Skillfully he drove her, higher and higher. To the edge of heaven, all the while stoking a mindless, consuming need inside her. Until, finally, she tumbled off that cloud of need into a glorious universe of twinkling, brilliant stars, and she cried out with the splendor of it. He took the same tumble seconds later, and she held him while he held her and they both trembled from the intensity of what they'd just shared.

Eventually, bracing his weight on his elbows, Digby rolled off her, settling her close beside him. Her hair draped over his shoulder like strands of silk. Her soft breasts were mounds of sheer pleasure crushing against his ribs. Compared to his size and strength, she was small and delicate, and yet...he was struck by the notion that she was more substantial than any woman he'd ever held in his arms.

Reluctantly, he eased his arm from beneath her head. "I've got to take care of—" He gestured.

She nodded comprehension.

Digby dropped his feet to the floor, then cocked his head around to look back at Keeley. Let the fools dropping coins in one-armed bandits and rolling dice downstairs wish for luck in the casino; he'd struck it luckier than any of them when he'd met Keeley Owens on his way into town. Leaning, he dropped a quick kiss on her cheek and drawled, "Don't even *think* about going anywhere."

"I wasn't," Keeley murmured, admiring the muscle play in his firm buttocks as he walked away from the bed. She didn't want to think, or move, or even talk. She just wanted to...*be*.

Right where she was.

In the bed of a man she'd met less than twelve hours ago.

But she didn't want to think about that, either. Under normal circumstances, on an ordinary day, winding up in bed with a man she hardly knew would have been unthinkable. But having sex with a near stranger was no more bizarre than any other in the long chain of events that had filled the hours since she'd gotten out of bed today.

She located her camisole and boxers and put them on. Then straightening the bedding, she turned back the sheets invitingly and settled back into bed. Boneless as a jellyfish, lethargic as an alligator sunning itself, she closed her eyes as her head slowly sank into the stiff hotel pillow. She had no right to feel this good, on the night following the worst day of her life. But their lovemaking had leeched every last snippet of tension from her body, leaving her physically drained but thoroughly relaxed. *Mellow* was the only word she could think of to describe her state of mind and body.

Hearing movement, she opened her eyes. Digby was returning to bed. And the only thing he was wearing was a smile. "For a moment there I thought you'd already drifted off."

"No. Not yet."

He got into bed and aligned his long body with hers, negotiating his arm beneath her neck as she cooperated. She turned slightly toward him as his weight tilted the bed in his direction. Settling her head on his shoulder, she stretched her arm across his waist and rested her leg, bent at the knee, on his hard thigh.

Digby kissed the top of her head. "Comfortable?"

"Uh-huh." She sighed. *Too* comfortable. *Oh, God, what was she doing here like this?* She lay there just savoring the tranquillity of being with a hard, strong man.

"You're awfully quiet," Digby said.

"Mmm," Keeley agreed, shifting slightly. She didn't want to talk. Not tonight. If she talked, she might start thinking. And if she started thinking...

"You've had a hell of a day," he said after an extended pause.

Keeley groaned softly. "I thought men didn't like to talk after sex."

His chuckle vibrated beneath her ear. "I thought women did."

"Not always."

A long silence followed. Digby drew a deep breath. "Keeley, are you...is everything...all right?"

"Mmm," she murmured. "I feel...*safe.*"

Digby was feeling many things at the moment, but "safe" wasn't one of them. "Unsettled" was more like it. He couldn't remember the last time a woman had turned his world upside down in so short a time. High school, maybe, if then. More than a little infatuated with Keeley, he'd be perfectly content to stay right where he was for the rest of his vacation as long as Keeley, wearing next to nothing, was pressed against him.

His vacation hadn't started out shabbily. No, not shabbily at all. Less than twelve hours after stepping off the plane in Vegas, he was in bed with a beautiful woman. And he'd worked out the problem with the assembler, to boot.

"What are we going to—" he was about to finish "—do tomorrow?" when he realized that Keeley's breathing had slowed, and her body was totally relaxed. Keeley Owens, feeling *safe*, was sound asleep.

Digby lifted her hand to his lips and kissed her fingertips, then replaced it on his chest before switching off the bedside lamp. Grinning in the darkness, he said softly, "I'm sure we'll think of something."

Keeley sighed in her sleep and snuggled closer to his warmth.

Ah, yes. They'd think of something. The possibilities were endless. He could think of quite a few already.

DIGBY AWOKE rested and alert. Keeley's back was wedged against his side, her soft bottom against his hip. He picked up a strand of her hair. It smelled like flowers and spice. He rubbed it between his fingers and brushed a curl over his cheek. The sleek, fine strands caught in the stubble of a night's growth of whiskers.

Keeley sighed and rolled over, then resettled with her breasts nestled against his ribs and her thigh aligned with his. The thought that he wouldn't mind waking up with Keeley Owens every morning flitted through his mind.

Digby grinned at his own folly. He'd been too long without a woman, obviously. He lay there, savoring the feel of her body touching his, until she shifted again and rolled back onto her side, stimulating every nerve ending in his body in the process. This woman was dynamite even when she was asleep!

Tentatively he brushed her hair from her neck and kissed her nape. She skipped a breath, but didn't rouse. As tempted as he was to wake her, he resisted the urge. After everything she'd been through yesterday, she deserved to rest.

Easing his arm from beneath her, he flexed it a few times to get his circulation back, then carefully got out of bed. He would shower, order up some breakfast and read the morning paper until Sleeping Beauty opened those pretty eyes. After that...

KEELEY WAITED until she heard the water running before making a dash for her **own ro**om, thanking her

lucky stars that he was a morning showerer. She
needed some time to think and considerably more
clothing than she was wearing before she was able to
face him again, knowing that they'd done what they'd
done last night. A one-night stand! She'd never had a
one-night stand in her life! Before Troy, there had
been...*no one.*

No one.

Then a man she was head over heels infatuated with,
and now—

A stranger. Practically.

Not anymore, toots! He's no stranger after last night!

She locked the door behind her, leaned against it
limply, buried her face in her hands and groaned.
From the way he'd been nibbling on the back of her
neck, he wanted to resume where they'd left off. And
as pleasant as it had been waking up with a *virile* man
nuzzling her neck, the light of day had brought with it
some portion of the sanity that seemed to have deserted her last night.

Not that it hadn't been...well, *nice.* It had been.

That was a large part of the problem, a complication
she didn't need. It was a perfectly understandable
thing to seek human comfort when she was upset, but
she'd gotten more than just comfort last night. He'd
said so when they were making love, and she couldn't
deny it.

She couldn't dwell on it, either, even if she'd wanted
to. She didn't have the luxury of time. She knew Digby
Barnes well enough to know that he would be banging
on the door as soon as he discovered she was gone, and
she wanted to be fully dressed and alert when she
faced him.

Quickly, she called the desk and asked if they could help her book a flight home on the next available flight. Then she retreated into the bathroom, closing the door and turning on the shower to drown out the sound of any knocking. Wielding her bath puff like sandpaper, she scrubbed until she was pink all over, then stood under the shower with her face tilted into the flow to let the water sluice over it.

Finally she stepped from the tub, patted herself dry and wrapped a towel around her. She was leaning over to step into her panties when a crashing, impatient knock disturbed the relative silence. "Keeley?"

As though he could see through the door, Keeley pulled the towel more securely around her. "I'm not dressed yet."

His belly laugh, smug and male, filtered through the door. "I can deal with that."

"I can't!"

"You did all right last night."

"Digby—"

"I hope you like omelettes. I've ordered breakfast."

"I—" Keeley drew in a breath and held it a moment.

"Clothing is optional."

"Digby, I—" She let out the breath in a rush of relief when the phone rang. "I have to answer the phone."

Digby leaned his broad back against the door, crossed his arms over his waist and muttered under his breath, "I'll wait."

What choice did he have? Frowning, he strained to hear her side of the conversation, but her occasional "um-huh" and "yes" offered few revelations about the oh so conveniently timed phone call. Damn, but women were unpredictable! The last thing he'd expected from her was this morning-after disappearing act.

"Yes. Yes. I have it. Thank you." The rustle of movement followed the click of the receiver being replaced. Then he heard Keeley dressing.

Involuntarily, Digby speculated on how much clothing she *hadn't* been wearing. Remembered the look and feel of her body. Imagined her sliding cloth over soft, smooth skin. Envisioned the fabric settling over flesh he'd touched and caressed.

He would have enjoyed watching her dress.

He would enjoy undressing her again. Making love to her again with the lights on. Watching her face as he found the right places to touch—

His fantasy was interrupted by the arrival of the room-service order. He let the waiter in, exchanged good mornings as the young man set the tray on the table, signed for the food and then sent the waiter off with a generous tip. A bud vase with a pink carnation and two sprigs of fern ornamented the tray. Digby took the flower and, holding it, walked to the connecting door. He raised his free hand to knock, but before his fist hit the door, it opened.

He and Keeley gasped in unison. Digby took advantage of her momentary immobility and dipped his mouth to hers for a brief kiss. Then, smiling, he presented the flower to her with the flourish of a magician who'd just produced it from thin air. "Good morning."

"T-thank you," she said, obviously still recovering from the surprise of their impromptu encounter. Her fingers were unsteady as she took the carnation, and her smile came with effort.

Digby eyed her from head to toe. "I see you decided to dress for breakfast." *Too bad.*

"I need to talk to you." Her seriousness ruled out idle chitchat.

He gestured to the table. "We can talk over our omelettes."

She gave a tight nod and walked past him, leading the way. When they were seated, she touched the tip of a fern frond and grinned. "So that's where you got a flower this early."

Digby nodded. "It had your name all over it."

Her grin segued into a genuine smile as she twirled the stem of the carnation between her thumb and forefinger. The smile brightened her face. She was wearing very little makeup, and her hair was loose. She looked pretty—wholesome and fresh—but Digby was afraid that if he told her so, she'd think he was giving her a line.

"May I?" he asked, reaching across the table to lift the metal dome lid from her plate before uncovering his own. Steam rich with the aroma of butter, eggs and cheese wafted up from a beautifully formed omelette. "It's still hot, obviously."

Keeley spread her napkin over her lap and said wistfully, "My grandmother used to make omelettes every Sunday morning."

"Did you live with your grandmother?"

"Yes." She hesitated, as though debating whether to go on. "My father left my mother when she was pregnant with me, so she went home to her parents' house. She never remarried, so that's where I grew up."

"Did you have any kind of contact with your father?"

"No," she said, shaking her head. "Once he left, he was long-gone."

"I can't imagine that. My dad and I have always been pals."

"I had my grandfather." Her gaze fell on the carnation beside her plate and held. "At least until I was twelve."

"He passed away?"

She nodded without looking up. "His heart."

"Too bad," Digby said.

"After that, it was just my mom, my grandmother and me—three hens without a rooster." An enigmatic smile lifted the corners of her mouth. "My grandmother always could turn a phrase or come up with an apt expression."

"She's still—" Digby stalled in midsentence. Was there a tactful way to ask if a person was still alive?

Keeley caught his meaning. "Oh, yes. She's very much with us."

Digby gambled a grin. "Your face lights up every time you mention her."

"Temperamentally, she and I are a lot alike. My mother never really got over my dad leaving her, and she—" She stopped abruptly, drew a fortifying breath then exhaled slowly. "I didn't come in here to bore you with my life story."

"You're not boring me." The sensual gleam in his eyes suggested that he was anything but bored. And that his mind was not fully focused on their conversation. "Just what did you come for?"

Keeley squared her shoulders, steeling herself against the seductive suggestion that flowed like liquid yearning in his voice. "To...thank you. And to tell you—" She emptied her lungs in a rush and then said, "I'm leaving. I'm going home. I have a ten-thirty flight."

"Ten-thirty? As in *a.m.*?" Everything about him telegraphed his displeasure—the set of his shoulders, his scowl-frown, the careful control in his voice. Combined with his imposing size, that almost palpable displeasure was disconcerting. "Two hours from now?"

Keeley nodded sheepishly.

"I was hoping we'd be able to spend some time together, get to know each other," he said.

Their eyes met and Keeley felt warmth rising in her cheeks as detailed memories of the closeness they'd shared the night before invaded the silence between them. *You already know me too well—much too well.*

"I have to get back to Florida," she told him. "I have to move out of my—out of *Troy's* apartment." She paused, then groaned. "I have to find someplace to move *to*, and pack, and—" *Rethink my future...rebuild my life.*

"If you took a couple of days—"

"No," she said sharply. "I have to do this *now*. Today. The sooner I get started, the better." *The sooner I get away from you, the sooner I'll be able to put last night into perspective. Last night, yesterday; the wedding that didn't happen, the casual sex that did. The casual sex that didn't seem casual, with the stranger who didn't seem like a stranger.* She'd read enough storybooks as a child to know that a rescued damsel was supposed to kiss the knight, but after that, things were a little fuzzy. Did a "kiss" include sleeping with him?

"I'll take you to the airport."

"It's a little too far for a piggyback ride, don't you think?"

"I was thinking more along the lines of a taxi," he said, then added playfully, "Not that the piggyback idea doesn't have some possibilities."

"There's a shuttle every twenty minutes," she said, ignoring the sexual innuendo. "I'll just catch the eight forty-five."

"But taxis have sentimental value," he said with a cajoling grin. "We could share some quality time in a taxi between here and the airport."

Keeley didn't doubt that. But she didn't trust him not to try to persuade her to stay in Vegas a few days longer, and she didn't trust herself not to be persuaded. She was confused enough already. She needed space. "You don't have to waste half a day of your vacation going back and forth to the airport with me," she said.

He reached across the table to cover her hand with his, commanding her attention. "I want to spend every minute I can with you."

Keeley found his intensity unsettling. It was too much, too quickly, too soon after Troy. And the scariest part was, she felt the same way. Or she could have, if she let herself.

Fortunately, she still had enough common sense left to know that what seemed like a dream last night might turn out to be a nightmare down the line. "Why don't you walk me down to the lobby and keep me company while I wait for the shuttle," she suggested. "You can carry my suitcase."

"Oh, sure. Carry your suitcase. I'm nothing but a convenient set of hard biceps to you."

"That's not true," she said, appalled that he would think such a thing. "I appreciate—" Embarrassed, she stopped as, too late, the teasing tone of his words registered as ironic humor.

"You women are all alike," he continued in the same ironic vein. "Sleep with a man, use him and then walk away without a backward glance." He pressed the back of his hand to his forehead in a melodramatic stage gesture and said in a tremulous falsetto, "I feel so cheap!"

As extraordinary as it was to hear Digby Barnes talking in a falsetto, the humorous quip hit too close to the way Keeley was feeling for her to find it truly funny. Choking back a lump of emotion, she stood abruptly. "I have a few more things to pack."

She was zipping her makeup bag after jamming in her toothbrush when she heard a soft knock. Exiting the bathroom, she found Digby standing in the doorway of the connecting door. He'd waited to be invited into her room before actually entering it, but he seemed to take her acknowledgment of his presence as invitation enough.

"I just had a brilliant idea," he said.

She looked at him expectantly.

"I have several days of vacation left and no plans to tie me down. I could go to Florida with you."

"You can't do that!" Keeley said.

Digby shrugged. "Nothing to it. Just hop a flight. You got a ticket this morning. That means the flight's probably not totally booked."

"It's out of the question. I have a million things to do when I get home."

"I could help. I'm a big, brawny guy—great with heavy boxes."

Brawny, yes. Way too brawny. Way too male. She couldn't deal with that right now. She had to put everything that had happened into perspective, including what had happened last night. "I don't even know where I'm going to move to yet."

"I'll help you look for a place."

"I...don't...think...so," Keeley said, separating the words into the current catchphrase to express incredulity. She wasn't about to let him poke his nose—or any other part of his anatomy—into her search for a new address.

"You shouldn't turn down experienced help," he said. "I've moved around a lot, so I know what to look for. I could give you the benefit of my experience."

She released a sigh that ended with her shoulders sagging before adding, "Give it up, Digby. It's a generous offer, but it's a bad idea."

"Last night—"

"Last night has nothing to do with it," she snapped. She'd known he was going to bring it up, and she wasn't ready to deal with it. "Forget last night."

"Sorry, sweetheart," Digby said, making what should have been a snide endearment seem personal and intimate. "I can't forget anything that incredible."

"Last night was a fluke!" she said.

"We don't know that," he said. "For all we know, the next time might be even more incredible, and the time after that—"

"I should have kept the damned door locked and pretended I didn't hear you knocking!" she grumbled, crossing her arms.

"Why?" Digby challenged. "So you could sneak off pretending we didn't make love last night?"

"Because I didn't want to have this conversation," she said. "I'm not *ready* to have this conversation." Frowning, she confessed, "I don't even know *how* to have this conversation. This was my first one-night stand."

"It doesn't have to be a one-night stand," Digby said.

"And if I stayed here with you, or you came to Florida with me, then what? Instead of a one-night stand, it could become a vacation fling?"

"Who knows what it might become if we spent some time together?"

Again, that intensity. Keeley didn't just hear it, she shared it. It hummed through her. But she couldn't trust her feelings now, not when she was still trying to deal with her breakup with Troy.

"Digby, last night—I won't forget it, either. But that woman who came into your room—that wasn't me. It was a confused, frightened woman whose world had just been turned upside down. A woman who was a long way from home and needed someone to hold on to."

"That might be who came to my bed, but she's not the woman I spent the night with. Keeley, last night wasn't just about sex."

He paused, waiting for her reaction. A denial? Agreement? An argument? "You're scaring me," she said.

"The truth is scaring you," he countered. "What you felt last night is scaring you."

"No!" she said, trying to make him understand that

she needed space. "It's you. I'm flattered that you wanted me to stay and share your vacation, but wanting to follow me back home is...it's obsessive."

Digby let out a chortle of stunned surprise. "It's *not* obsessive for a man to want to spend some time with a woman."

"Maybe not," Keeley said. "But when a man wants to follow a woman he hardly knows three-quarters of the way across the nation, it's more like *stalking*."

"That does it!" he said, throwing his hands in the air. "Forget I even suggested it." He shook his head. "Stalking!" Then, gesturing to the suitcase on the luggage rack, he said sharply, "Is that bag ready to go?"

Keeley nodded and he picked it up. "Then let's get moving. You have a shuttle to catch."

Keeley grabbed her makeup kit and handbag and hurried after him, struggling to keep up with his long strides. He'd already punched the button to summon the elevator. They were the only two people waiting, and for a full minute, they stood side by side exchanging surreptitious glances.

Finally, Keeley couldn't stand it any longer. She hadn't meant to hurt his feelings. She tried to explain. "When I get home, one of the things I have to do—the *main* thing—is put everything that happened here into perspective. I can't do that if you're there."

Digby shifted his weight from one foot to the other. "You made your point."

The elevator arrived and they stepped inside.

"I don't really think you're a stalker," Keeley said softly as the car descended.

Digby frowned. "Women are always complaining

that men disappear after sleeping with them. And then, when a man tries to keep in touch—"

The elevator squeaked to a stop and the doors opened. Digby took Keeley's suitcase to the curb while Keeley checked out. He was waiting for her near the valet stand when she exited the lobby.

"They're expecting the shuttle any minute," he informed her. Cupping her elbow, he guided her into a small alcove behind a desert boulder–motif planter filled with cacti. "We might as well wait out here."

He turned so they were facing each other and, suddenly, when it was about to end, Keeley was struck with a realization of how much had happened between them—and how many ways he had helped her through a hellish interlude in her life. How had she ever thought his face severe, when his eyes were so eloquently expressive? The way he was looking at her aroused every female atom in her. She had to say something, and quickly, or she might just spontaneously combust with the awareness of his virility. She swallowed. "Thanks again for rescuing me."

His gaze locked with hers. "It was entirely my pleasure."

His inflection of the word *pleasure* imbued it with a sexual connotation that brought color to Keeley's cheeks. After a lengthy pause, he said, "I don't suppose it would do any good to try to talk you out of leaving."

Keeley shook her head instead of speaking, afraid her voice might betray the fact that she was half an impulse away from skipping the flight. The prospect of a mad holiday in his company was infinitely more appealing than that of a frantic quest for a new place to live. But it was more than dread of the task ahead that made her long to stay in Las Vegas with Digby. The intimacy they'd shared had forged a link between them. She would have been foolish to try to deny, even to herself, that she was emotionally involved with him, as well as physically attracted to him.

And that was just one more good reason she had to leave. She'd had enough spontaneity for a lifetime with Troy. She didn't need to get tangled up with another man who had a problem with making a commitment. Or reservations. She needed a man who was stable and grounded in reality. Dreamers and schemers need not apply.

Or tinkerers. What good was all that hulking virility when a woman was ready for a real relationship?

He capped her shoulders with his huge hands. "I shouldn't be saying goodbye to you."

"I'm going to miss you," she said, so mystified by the realization that she spoke before actually deciding to express the sentiment aloud.

"I—" He stopped, then growled, "Oh, hell!" Firming his grip on her shoulders, he pulled her close and lowered his head before she even realized he was going to kiss her.

He was in total control of the kiss from the moment their lips touched, demanding without forcing, taking what she freely surrendered; demanding more and taking that, too. They were so totally involved in the kiss—in each other—that they were unaware of the shuttle's arrival until the valet cleared his throat loudly. They drew back to gape in unison at the young man, who managed to keep a straight face as he said, "Excuse me, but the shuttle's here. Do you want your bag loaded?"

Keeley felt Digby's gaze on her face as he waited for her reply along with the valet. She sucked in a deep breath before replying, "Yes. Please. Of course. I'll be right there."

The valet nodded discreetly and turned away to take care of the bag.

"For a moment there, I thought you'd changed your mind," Digby said, and then grinned sheepishly. "Wishful thinking, I guess."

Still slightly disoriented from the effects of the kiss, Keeley stammered, "I—I—" She gestured toward the van parked at the curb.

Digby nodded resolutely and walked her to the vehicle. The van was filled almost to capacity. An older woman sitting next to the window primly gathered the full skirt of her print dress onto her own side of the seat to make room for Keeley.

Digby stood half-in and half-out of the sliding side door while the driver loaded the bags. "I don't have your phone number."

"I don't have one," Keeley said. "I won't until I get a place to live."

"I'll give you mine," he said. He slapped at a nonexistent breast pocket on his knit shirt and grumbled in frustration. "I don't have a pen!"

"Here," said a passenger in the row behind Keeley's, holding out a pen.

Anticipating the next crisis, Keeley ripped a deposit slip from her checkbook just as the driver walked to the side of the van to close the door. Taking the deposit slip with his left hand, Digby held up his right hand to stay the driver.

"I'm running close," the driver said. "These people have planes to catch."

"Thirty seconds," Digby pleaded, already scribbling frantically.

The driver frowned.

"Okay. Done," Digby said, pressing the paper into Keeley's hands and talking around the door as the door slid closed. "Leave a message if I don't pick up. Leave your new number!"

Keeley nodded, but she couldn't be sure he'd seen her—any more than she could be sure she was going to dial the number on the piece of paper she held clutched in her hand.

"That's a strapping young man," the woman next to her observed.

"Yes," Keeley agreed. "He's big, all right."

"My granddaughter would say he's a hunk."

"We...uh, just met. Here in Las Vegas," Keeley said. "He's very...nice. We went to a show last night." *And then I slept with him.*

"He seems quite taken with you."

Keeley pondered the woman's observation a moment. "He lives in Indiana, and I live in Florida. I don't think—" She ended the sentence with a sigh.

"You never can tell," the woman said. "Sometimes..."

Keeley took advantage of the woman's hesitation to ask, "Is this your first trip to Las Vegas?"

"Oh, I'm not a tourist. I live here. My son dropped me off at the hotel on his way to work. It's a nicer place to have breakfast than the airport, and the shuttle is convenient. I'm going to visit my daughter and my newest grandbaby in Houston."

"A new grandbaby?" Keeley said, relieved to have changed the subject. She didn't want to think about Digby Barnes just yet. She didn't want to think about Troy, either, or having been stranded on the highway, or about having to move with no advance planning. She'd have to deal with all of it when she got off the plane in Orlando. For now—

For now, she just wanted to leave the past and the future to fend for themselves.

"Do you have any pictures of the baby?" she asked, and spent the rest of the drive oohing and aahing over the woman's new grandson.

7

THE ONLY TIME Keeley had ever gone apartment hunting was when she moved to Orlando to enroll at the
university after finishing community college in Lake-
view. The hunting had been an adventure then. This
time, it was a pain in the posterior.

Already disenchanted with the entire situation in
which she found herself—the desperate necessity to
find a place *immediately*, the small-town girl in her
quickly wearied of the cookie-cutter city fare. By the
time she'd walked through empty units in three different complexes, she had formed the opinion that one
apartment was pretty much like any other. There were
differences—a window above the sink, a convenient
route into and out of traffic, a built-in desk off the
kitchen—but the overall ambience was the same in all
of them: urban crackerbox.

After leaving the fourth prospective complex, she
decided to go by the store and say hello to the owner,
Anne, who had come out of semiretirement to run the
store while Keeley was on vacation. She wanted to ask
if Anne's son, Michael, a high-school sophomore,
might be willing to help with the heavy lifting. Mike
worked part-time at the shop, providing muscle whenever needed.

Approaching from an unfamiliar direction, she gambled a turn onto a street that she hoped would connect

her with the highway on which the shop was located. Instead, it wound into a quiet neighborhood of charming little houses, many of them block construction that reminded her of her grandmother's house. They were older homes, most set well back on tree-shaded lawns, with open carports instead of garages.

She could hardly believe her eyes when she saw a hand-lettered For Lease sign in one of the yards. Was it karma? Fate? Just plain old good luck? She turned into the driveway and parked, taking a close look at the house. It was a simple rectangle with a bank of steps leading to a narrow porch that ran the full width of the front. All the windows were shuttered.

All the windows were shuttered!

She jotted down the phone number on the sign, hoping the house was within her price range. Maybe, since it was old and small...

She backed to the end of the driveway and was waiting for a car to pass in the street, when she caught sight of movement near the house. A woman dressed in typical Florida day wear, knit shorts and shirt and sneakers, was running toward her from the neighboring yard, waving her arms. Keeley rolled down the window as the woman approached the car.

"Are you Marnie's friend?" the woman asked, still on the move.

"No," Keeley said. "I...I don't know anyone named Marnie."

"Oh," the woman said, heaving from exertion. "Oh, I see. My beautician said she knew someone who might be interested in the house and she might drop by around noon. I assumed she'd changed her mind, but when I heard the car—"

"I was just driving past and saw the sign."

"Would you like to see the house?"

"Now?"

The woman shrugged. "If you want to see it and have the time, you might as well take a look now."

Keeley turned off the engine and grabbed her handbag. "I'm dying to see it."

"The rooms are small and the closets are smaller, but the floors are in good shape and the kitchen was totally overhauled a few years ago."

"Are you the owner?"

"I don't know where my manners are," the woman said with a chuckle. She was wearing no makeup, and her short hair had been permed and thereafter left to its own inclinations, but her laugh was cheery and her blue eyes were bright. "I'm Mildred. I live next door and manage the house for the owner."

Keeley introduced herself, and gave the house an evaluative perusal. "I really hadn't thought about renting a house. I've been looking at apartments."

"I like having a yard, myself," Mildred said. "And a little space between my walls and the neighbors'." She led Keeley up the steps and into the house. "Do you have children?"

"No," Keeley said. "I'm not married." *Although I could have been,* she thought incredulously. Las Vegas already seemed more like a movie she'd seen than events she'd lived. "I'll be living alone." *For the first time in my life.*

"This is the living room, obviously," Mildred said. "The kitchen's this way," Mildred said. "Refrigerator's old, but it works great. And that top oven is a microwave. It was part of the renovation."

"I like the window over the sink," Keeley said, watching a squirrel scamper up a tree.

"It's nice to have something to see when you're working," Mildred agreed. "There's no formal dining room, but this breakfast nook is large enough for a big table and a china hutch."

"No formal dining room is not a problem," Keeley said. "I don't even have a dinette set yet."

"You could have some fun fixing it up, then," Mildred said. She paused, giving Keeley time to envision the room all furnished, before saying, "The bedrooms are this way."

There was one door on the right side of the hallway, one at the very end and two on the left. Mildred turned right. "This is the master bedroom. A kingsize bed nearly fills it up, but if you have a smaller size—"

"I have a single," Keeley said. The mattress and springs were in the back of the walk-in closet in Troy's apartment, where she'd put them when she moved in and began sharing Troy's water bed.

"The bathroom's right out here," Mildred said, going back into the hall. "There's just the one. A lot of people can't deal with that, especially the ones with children." She shook her head. "When I was a little girl, we were lucky to have a bathroom inside the house instead of in the backyard."

"Everything looks like it's in good shape," Keeley said.

"Edith—the owner of the house—is a scrupulous housekeeper. She and Dan moved into this house the same month Al and I moved into ours. We raised our children together, played cards or dominoes on Friday nights and swapped gossip for almost forty years." She choked back a lump of emotion. "Dan passed away year before last, and Edith moved up to Atlanta, to be near her children."

She sighed again. "The other two bedrooms are over here."

Keeley stuck her head in each of the rooms. "You were right. They're very small." Then she smiled broadly. "But I love the house. I want it if I can afford it."

The rent was comparable to that of the apartments she'd been pricing. Relieved, she said, "How soon can I move in?"

Mildred's expression was somber, cautious. "The house is ready, obviously, but—" She shifted uncomfortably. "You seem like a sweet girl, but I have to tell you, this is a quiet neighborhood, and we like it that way."

"I'm not a party animal," Keeley said. *Not anymore.* She'd had enough of that with Troy.

"I didn't think so," Mildred said. "But I didn't want any misunderstandings." She paused. "If you fill out the application now, I can check your references this afternoon, and you can start moving in tomorrow."

Keeley filled out the necessary papers and then drove to the store. Anne was taking an order for personalized napkins for a wedding reception when Keeley walked in. She looked up briefly and raised an eyebrow inquisitively. Keeley mouthed that she would talk to her after the customer was gone and took a leisurely stroll around the store while she waited for Anne to finish with the prospective bride and groom.

It was hard to believe she'd been away from the

store only a few days. She turned as Anne approached. "You did a great job on this Halloween display."

"Thanks." Anne replied. Then, "I thought you were in Las Vegas."

"I came back early. I'm...moving."

"Into a house," Anne said, and then grinned. "A woman just called to verify that you're the manager here. Then she asked for me, specifically, and wanted to know if you were reliable. She said you were interested in a house and had listed me as a reference."

"I hope you don't mind."

"No. Of course not, but—" She seemed puzzled. "She said you said you would be living alone."

Keeley took a deep breath and nodded. "Troy and I broke up. I came back early so I could move out of the apartment before he gets back."

"When I heard you were looking at a house, I thought maybe you and Troy had decided to tie the knot in Vegas."

"We did," Keeley said.

"You got married? I thought you said—"

"That's just it. We *didn't* get married."

"Well—I'm totally confused," Anne said wryly.

Keeley heaved a deep breath and then told her friend the whole sordid story about Troy winning the money and going to the chapel and her sudden realization that Troy was all wrong for her.

"What a relief!" Anne said. "I thought you'd never wake up and smell the coffee where he was concerned."

Keeley was shocked. "You didn't like Troy?"

"It's not a question of liking him. He just never struck me as husband material, especially for you."

"Why not?" She'd adored Troy from the moment she'd met him. It had never occurred to her, even as their relationship had gone into a steady decline, that not every woman would see him as a prize.

"Because you and he are total opposites, of course."

"Opposites?" Keeley had never thought of herself and Troy as opposites, but as different types who complemented each other.

"Keeley, you're probably the most genuine person I've ever met."

The answer wasn't what Keeley had been anticipating. "And Troy?"

Anne turned up her palms in a what-can-I-do-it's-the-truth gesture and said flatly, "Troy isn't."

"Not genuine?" She mulled over the idea in her mind.

"Come on, Keeley. Troy has to be the center of attention. He's always 'on,' and he surrounds himself with people he knows will keep him there—including you."

Keeley wanted to deny what Anne was saying, but she couldn't. Troy *did* like the spotlight; and, she now realized, she *had* helped to keep him there. "I guess I always believed he belonged there."

Anne chuckled. "That was one thing you two had in common: you both wanted Troy to have exactly what Troy wanted."

"I guess we still do," Keeley confessed. "He was pretty adamant about my being out of the apartment by the time he gets back, and that's what I'm trying to do."

"So tell me about your house," Anne said.

Keeley brightened. "Oh, Anne, it's an absolute dollhouse. I was in such a stew about getting out of the apartment that I wasn't even thinking I'd find a place I would enjoy. But I turned down a side street trying to find the highway and there it was."

"Voila!" Anne said.

"Voila!" Keeley agreed.

"So when do I get to see it?"

"I'll start moving in tomorrow. I was hoping you and Michael—"

"You know it!" Anne said. She fixed a motherly eye on Keeley. "So how are you—really? Are you okay with all of this?"

"I know I should be falling apart," Keeley said, "but it's been sinking in by degrees." Relief mingled with shock. Acceptance mingled with sadness. "In a way, what he pulled—leaving me stranded like that—made it easier to let go."

"Stranded?"

"In the desert," Keeley said, downplaying the incident. "After I left the chapel. I had to get a cab to get back to the hotel." *And I was rescued by a giant.*

"What a prince!" Anne said.

Keeley had been thinking of Digby, so she was slow to realize that Anne's sarcastic barb was aimed at Troy. "Oh—well, I lived through it. You know what they say—what doesn't kill us makes us stronger."

She could tell the attempt at whimsical irony had fallen short of success. Although she had not exactly lied to Anne, she'd deliberately omitted a significant element of the story. But she wasn't ready to talk about Digby. She wasn't sure she ever would be. It might be something she tucked away in her heart and never shared with anyone. Except Digby. She was trying to put the entire—*affair*, for lack of a better word—into perspective and she was having a little trouble doing so. Just as Digby seemed a bit out of proportion because of his sheer physical size, their encounter seemed a bit out of proportion in her life, an extraordinary interlude in an otherwise ordinary life. "I just hope..." She let her voice trail off.

"You're not hoping he'll come home and beg you to stay?" Anne's concern was evident.

"No," Keeley assured her, relieved at a new twist in the conversation. "I don't want that. Troy and I are *kaput. Finis.* I just hope that we can act civilized."

"Don't count on it," Anne said. "That man has an ego the size of a third-world country, and you embarrassed him in front of his cheering section."

"I just want to be out of the apartment before he gets back," Keeley said. "Speaking of which—are there any empty boxes in the back room?"

"You're in luck," Anne said. "I unpacked all those papier-mâché pumpkins yesterday. Michael broke down the boxes, and they're stacked back there neat as a pin. There must be a dozen of them."

An electronic giggle, followed inevitably by a jolly-clown voice saying, "Come on in. We'll have a party!" signaled the arrival of two customers. Keeley and Anne reflexively looked toward the door.

"Duty calls," Anne said, turning to greet the women who'd entered.

Keeley went to the storage room and gathered the boxes, then lugged them to her car, nodding a farewell to Anne, who was showing a customer the baby-shower decorations.

KEELEY SPENT more than an hour on her farewell note to Troy. Although she felt like one vacillating bundle of emotions, when she sat down to put pen to paper, she found it hard to express everything she wanted— needed—to say. She did not want to sound maudlin, bitter, petty or bitchy. In the end, she opted for direct- ness, brevity and simplicity. She told him that the time they'd been together had been meaningful to her and thanked him for the memories she would always cher- ish. She wished him happiness and said she hoped he would remember her as fondly as she would remem- ber him. Four sentences, and then, "Fondly" and her name. Her first name only.

After sealing the short letter, along with her key to the apartment, into an envelope and writing Troy's name on the front, she deliberated where to leave it. A mantel would have been perfect, but there was no fire- place in the apartment. Pinning it to the pillow would have been too intimate. Sticking it to the front of the re- frigerator with a magnet seemed tacky and insignifi- cant for so important a letter. She even considered the bathroom mirror, but that was just too dramatic and inappropriate. Bathroom mirrors were for sexy mes- sages from enchanted lovers and ominous threats writ- ten in blood by psychopathic murderers; departing "main squeezes" did not leave formal goodbye notes on them.

Ultimately, she left the note on the small table near the door where whoever brought in the mail put the other's letters and bills. The pale yellow envelope stood out on the stack of accumulated mail, conspicu- ous as a gold nugget in a pile of sand.

It was the last thing she looked at before setting the door to lock behind her and leaving the apartment for the last time. Everything she owned was sitting in the house she'd leased, waiting to be unpacked.

She'd spent the past two days going through the apartment—Troy's apartment—room by room, wall by wall, drawer by drawer, agonizing over what to take and what to leave, trying to be both practical and just, leaving anything she thought Troy might conceivably need, want or miss, and taking anything she particularly needed or wanted.

Each item requiring a decision had a memory attached—a shopping trip to the mall or flea market, an art show on Church Street, a party they'd attended. She'd taken the videos of movies she liked and left him the action-adventures he favored, taken the wine goblets and left him the highball tumblers from the set of glasses they'd picked out together.

The process had left her emotionally drained, mourning the end of the relationship, regretting that it couldn't last even as she became convinced that the breakup had been inevitable.

She allowed herself no backward glances as she drove away. The apartment was her past. Her future was waiting for her in her new home, waiting to be embraced.

Along with all those boxes waiting to be unpacked.

Even with the cartons cluttering the rooms, when Keeley entered the house knowing it was now her home, she was struck by how underfurnished it was. She owned a rocking chair, a television set, a shelf to put it on, a twin bed and a chest of drawers. Even in a small house, they were like tiny goldfish in a huge aquarium.

Tonight she would unpack and organize.

Tomorrow she would shop.

Having made the definitive plans for the immediate future, she set about making the house livable: towels in the bathroom, sheets on the bed, her alarm clock-telephone on the table beside it. She was relieved to hear the dial tone when she plugged in the phone, glad the telephone company had activated the service as promised. She wouldn't have relished spending the first night in a strange place with no link to the outside world.

After testing the phone, she was hit by a mischievous urge to call someone. But who? The store, to let Anne know she was now officially moved into the house? Anne already knew.

Her grandmother. She'd promised her grandmother she'd let her know her new address and phone number as soon as she was settled.

She reached for the receiver—and nearly jumped in surprise when the phone rang. It rang a second time as she released the lungful of air she'd gasped. It was probably the phone company, checking to see that the line was functioning properly. Thinking they must have some sort of signal when the phone is first plugged in, she picked up the receiver. "Hello."

"You're home!"

Keeley didn't recognize the voice. "I believe you must have the wrong number," she said.

"Keeley?"

An tingle rose up her spine as the voice registered. And then her heart sped up with excitement. "Digby?"

8

"I WAS BEGINNING to think you'd forgotten me," Digby said.

"No," Keeley said. "I...just...wasn't expecting the phone to ring."

"I've been trying to get you all afternoon."

"The phone wasn't plugged in yet."

"So you really moved."

"I've moved *out* of the apartment, but I've barely begun to move *in*," she said. And then, curiously, she asked, "How did you get this number?"

"I could tell you, but then I'd have to kill you," he quipped with a chuckle. *Did she think he'd pulled strings at the Central Intelligence Agency?*

"Seriously," she said.

"I called directory assistance and asked if there was a new listing, of course." *And breathed a lot easier when there was one.* He'd been afraid she might hang around for the boyfriend to get back before moving out. And there was always the chance the boyfriend would come back carrying a bouquet of roses.

"I'm surprised they already have the number."

"It's computerization," Digby said. "The number probably popped on-line electronically when the service was activated."

"Um," Keeley agreed absently.

Digby shifted restlessly. He hadn't called to talk about computers and directory information.

"Are you still in Vegas?" she asked.

"Yes." He paused a second or two, then added, "But it's boring without you."

"Surely you could find some damsels in need of rescuing."

"I haven't been in a rescuing mood since you left." The glitz and noise and overall rowdy ambience of the city had been wasted on him. He'd gone through the motions, played nickel poker in the slot machines until his arm was sore from pulling the handles, and breathed enough secondhand smoke to give him a scratchy throat, but the only excitement he'd found in the city had come packaged in sexy white lace. Everything he'd done since she'd left had been anticlimactic.

Literally.

"So how are you?" he asked bluntly, unsettled by her silence.

"I'm—" She hesitated, as though she wasn't quite sure how she was, and then she said, "I'm okay," as though she'd just come to that conclusion. "I've stayed too busy to think. It's a great way to get through a crisis. I heartily recommend it."

"Did you have any trouble finding a place?" *Did you have second thoughts about splitting up with the boyfriend?*

Laughter tinkled through the line and danced over his senses. "Not much," she said. "I took a shortcut. Literally. I was driving down an unfamiliar street and there was a sign in the yard. Not a sign, like a *sign* from on high, although it seemed that way—but a For Lease sign in front of a darling little house."

Wishing she were next to him instead of so many

miles away on the other end of a phone, he adjusted the pillow under his neck to a more comfortable angle and let her go on and on about the "darling little house," "mmming" occasionally to let her know he was listening. It was good to hear her so animated. And even more gratifying to hear her going gaga over the house she'd be living in—without that jerk who'd left her standing beside the highway.

"I don't have much furniture, so it's almost empty," she said. "But that's okay. This is my first solo place. It's exciting to think that I can do whatever I want with the entire house—anything I can afford, anyway—without worrying about whether or not anyone else likes it. I'm going to enjoy fixing it up the way I want it."

He groaned teasingly. "I sense a wave of sunflowers and lace coming on."

"Sunflowers, definitely," she replied. "And maybe a touch of lace here and there in the bedrooms. I'm actually going to have a guest room."

Digby perked up. Keeley Owens's guest room was an idea pregnant with potential, if he'd ever heard one.

"A warm refuge for poor, frozen Northerners?" he hinted hopefully.

He heard the halting hesitation on the other end of the line as she tried to be tactful. "I've been trying to get my grandmother to come see the parks," she said evasively. "She wouldn't even consider staying overnight when...she didn't exactly approve of my living with Troy. Now, since I'll be in a house of my own—"

"I've been thinking about you." *Constantly. Wondering what was going on between her and that charmer of a boyfriend of hers.* "I want...I *need* to see you again."

He hadn't planned on being so blunt, but he didn't regret the spontaneous declaration. He wasn't a patient man by nature, and he despised playing games. He waited for a reaction.

"The silence coming from your end of the line is depressing," he said.

"Digby—"

"I hate it when you say my name that way."

"What way?"

"You know *what* way. Like a doctor about to tell me the condition is terminal."

Though she didn't answer right away, he sensed her dismay almost as though he were in the same room with her. "The tests aren't back from the lab yet," she said finally. And then, with blatant frustration, she snapped, "I don't know what to say to you, Digby. What happened in Las Vegas—"

"We made love."

"We had sex," she said.

"Very good sex."

"We had a one-night stand!"

"It wouldn't have been a one-night stand if you hadn't shot out of town like a hare with a hound on its trail."

"It wouldn't have happened at all if I hadn't been so vulnerable."

Another silence stretched through the line. The lack of sound emanating from Miss Keeley Owens's end was beginning to grate on Digby's nerves. And he didn't like the implication of her last statement. "Don't *even* try to suggest that I took advantage of you, sweetheart! I may have left the door unlocked, but you're the one who walked through it!" *Women!*

"I wasn't suggesting anything. I just...I'm having a little trouble putting what happened into perspective." She exhaled a sigh that managed to sound sensuous as it carried electronically through the wires. "If you must know, I haven't walked through all that many doors."

And that doesn't tell you that what happened was extraordinary? Digby frowned in sheer frustration. "I know you haven't. I was with you, remember? Don't you realize that only made it more meaningful?"

"Meaningful?" she said, sounding uncomfortable. "Digby...I needed to...*connect* that night. I needed someone to hold me, and you were there, and you were...kind and...you seemed to sense..." She paused to draw breath. "The fact that we...that *you* were there, and we—"

"Connected?" He couldn't help taking a little perverse pleasure in her discomfort. She was fighting what had happened between them too much for their being together to have been a mere fluke. They'd *connected* even before she'd walked through the door; even before he had kissed her good-night and left her in her own room.

"I don't want to talk about this," she said. "Not now, and...not over the phone."

"Agreed," Digby said. "So let's table it for now."

Again, she answered with silence. Which, to Digby's way of thinking, beat hostility, but barely. "So tell me what you're going to do to this house of yours," he said.

Keeley told him about using one of the bedrooms as a library-office; about using a seashell theme in the bathroom, about wanting a butcher-block table with hunter green ladder-back chairs in the breakfast nook, about hoping to develop a homey ambience in the living room around one of the few pieces of furniture she owned, a rocking chair.

"So," Digby said wryly, "other than that, what else are you going to do with your spare time for the next four or five years?"

Keeley chuckled. "Get a puppy?"

"Seriously?"

"I'm thinking about it," she said. "It would be good protection."

"Is your house in a crime-prone area?"

Keeley found his concern, so spontaneous and genuine, endearing. And so typically male. But then, Digby Barnes was nothing if not a prime example of pure manhood.

You ought to know! she thought, shifting uncomfortably.

"No more than any other area," she said. "I want one mostly for the company. I've missed Scooby since I left home."

"Scooby?" he teased.

"My best friend and I used to watch Scooby Doo every day after school."

"Great Dane?"

"No. Just a little mutt. We should have named him Scruffy instead of Scooby." She paused. "I've been wanting a dog, but Troy wasn't into that kind of commitment."

"Good thing you didn't want a baby."

"Who says I didn't?" Keeley said.

"Oh," Digby said, comprehending immediately. "So that's the way it was."

"The subject came up a few times," Keeley said. "It

wasn't a big issue yet." She sighed. "I don't want to talk about Troy. Troy's history."

Not yet, Digby thought. His greatest fear was that Keeley would have a change of heart about Sir Troy. Everything she told him that indicated there were insurmountable problems in the relationship helped alleviate that fear, but he wasn't going to breathe easy until Troy was back in town and he and Keeley continued to occupy separate residences. Until then, Troy wasn't history in her life, he was just on hold. No matter how ugly things had gotten between them in Vegas, Digby didn't see a man with an ego like Troy's letting go of a woman who'd walked out on him. He'd be wanting to prove to her and the entire world, and especially to himself, that he could charm her anytime he wanted.

Resist, Keeley, he thought. *Don't fall for it. Don't give in. If you do, we'll both end up with a broken heart. You'll break mine when you go back to him, and he'll break yours to prove he can do it.*

"I really need to get back to unpacking," she said.

Digby knew a dismissal when he heard one. Reluctantly, he said, "And I have to get packed up. I've got an early flight tomorrow."

Awkward silence. Then, timidly, from her end of the line, "Thank you for calling."

"Did you think I wouldn't? After what happened between us?"

"I—we live so far apart."

"In the world of phones, faxes and electronic mail, there's no such thing as far apart. Although—"

"Although...what?" she prompted after a beat of silence.

"If I'm going to reach out and touch you, it would be nice to do it the old-fashioned way—with hands and lips and—"

"Digby!"

"You were thinking the same thing I was thinking," he teased.

"I wasn't thinking anything."

Digby laughed. "If you weren't, you wouldn't be denying it."

"Goodbye, Digby."

"Just keep right on thinking about it," he said.

"I'm going to hang up now, Digby." The phone clicked.

"Goodbye, Keeley," Digby said to the dead line. He was grinning from ear to ear as he hung up the phone, but the grin gradually faded as he became newly aware of how far away she was.

"You could miss me a little," he said, speaking the wish into the room that had seemed empty ever since she'd left his bed.

KEELEY WAS PROCESSING a shipment of Thanksgiving items when the storage-room door opened. Another problem on the sales floor? Her first day back on the job had been a doozy, with one crisis after another.

"What now?" she lamented, looking up, expecting to see either Trish, the full-time clerk, or Anne's son, Michael, who was working on clearing shelf space for the Thanksgiving exhibit.

But the person who walked into the room was neither Trish nor Michael. He entered the room with a self-conscious smile on his handsome face and sheepishly thrust a bouquet of daisies in her direction. "Hi, Keeley."

Keeley hesitated a few seconds before taking the flowers. She didn't smile. "Hello, Troy."

"Bummer of a vacation, wasn't it?"

"That's putting it mildly."

Keeley had been uncertain how she would react when she saw him again, and she would have been hard-pressed to express what she was feeling. But there was one thing she was sure of: she was not in any danger of succumbing to a combination of nostalgia and his charm and falling back into his arms. She recognized his contriteness for what it was—a charming act of manipulation. How had it taken her so long to see through him?

"You really gut-punched me when you stopped the wedding that way."

"One of us had to do it," Keeley said. "And you were too drunk."

"Yeah. I guess winning all that money went to my head."

"Winning all that money and about a dozen tequila blitzes."

He tucked his head contritely. "I guess I was kinda rough on you."

"I guess you were more than 'kinda' rough on me," Keeley said.

"It was the booze talking."

"Booze seems to be doing a lot of your talking lately."

"Don't start ragging on me about that," he said. "We were on vacation. We were supposed to be having fun."

A lengthy silence followed. Keeley didn't reply; she didn't see any point in it. What purpose would arguing with him serve?

Finally, Troy shifted uncomfortably. "I found your note."

Keeley nodded mutely.

"You didn't say where you're staying."

"I didn't think it was important."

Troy mulled that over for a few seconds. "So where are you staying?"

"I'm not *staying* anywhere, Troy. I rented a house. I'm *living* there."

"You rented a house?"

"Yes. In a neighborhood. With a front and back yard and a window over the kitchen sink."

Troy looked as though he'd been gut-punched again. "You didn't sign a lease, did you?"

"Yes, I signed a lease. It's a house, not a hotel room."

"You really moved out."

Her gaze met his. "You told me you wanted me to, I told you I would. So, I did."

"Just like that?" he asked, snapping his fingers in the air.

"It's not 'just like that,'" she said. "It's been coming a long time. What happened in Las Vegas just brought it out in the open. You don't want to marry me, Troy."

"Hell, Keeley, just because we don't want to get married doesn't mean you have to move out."

"We want different things, Troy. I'm not going to change my mind about wanting a home and a family, and I'm not going to hang around in some kind of limbo waiting to see if you'll ever change yours."

Troy's expression turned ugly. Keeley knew him

well enough to recognize hurt along with the anger marring his beautiful features and flushing his cheeks. The interval before he spoke seemed to go on forever until, at last, he said, "It's that guy, isn't it? The one whose shirt you were wearing."

"He has nothing to do with what's happened between us," Keeley said. *I wouldn't even have met him if you hadn't left me stranded.*

"You slept with him!" Troy accused. "You slept with him, and he has your mind all screwed up about us."

Keeley refused to dignify his raised voice or the ugly assertion with a denial. Instead, calmly, she said, "How's Suzzi?"

"Suzzi's a bitch."

I could have told you that the moment she showed up on Cork's arm, Keeley thought, but she let the remark pass without comment. She watched his face while he stewed in rage and confusion.

"I wouldn't have paid any attention to Suzzi if you hadn't walked out on me the way you did."

You would have paid enough attention to know she was paying attention to you, Keeley thought. *You always have to know that people are paying attention to you. And no matter what happened, if it was bad, it was my fault.*

If, in the innermost hidden cranny of her heart, she'd still harbored doubts about breaking up with Troy, those last dregs of doubt melted away. And with their dissolution came a new freedom, a new confidence.

"Aren't you even going to say anything?" he shouted.

"I said everything I needed to say in the note," Keeley said with a soft tone of finality.

"I said everything I needed to say in the note," he

mocked loudly, his face twisted in disdain. "Aren't you uppity all of a sudden. Since when do we write notes?"

"Troy, please," Keeley said. "We've said everything there is to say, and this isn't the time or place—"

The door swung open then, and Anne entered, followed closely by Michael. "What's going on in here? I walked in the door and I could hear you from the front counter."

"Do you need any help, Keeley?" Michael asked, his hands balled into fists.

Keeley couldn't hold back a gentle smile at the boy's protectiveness. "No," Keeley said, fixing her gaze on Troy's face. "Troy was just leaving."

Troy's scowl would have scared small children. "Yeah. I'm leaving." His eyes narrowed in Keeley's direction. "There's nothing here worth fighting over." He turned to leave, but paused on his way out to cast a dirty look at Michael. Then, with a shake of his head, he turned his vitriolic glare on Keeley. "You just got them coming out of the woodwork these days, don't you? First that goon in Vegas and now the boss's kid." He shook his head again and gave an ugly laugh. "You did me a favor walking out on me."

"I did us both a favor," Keeley said to Troy's retreating back.

Dead silence followed. Slowly, Keeley became aware that both Anne and Michael were staring at her. Her face heated in a flush of embarrassment.

"I—" she said, then sighed before starting over. "I'm sorry this happened here. Troy just showed up."

Anne shrugged. "Forget Troy—I want to hear more about the *goon* in Vegas."

9

DIGBY OPENED the file folder and lined up the contents on the top of his desk. Each bundle of papers represented a potential project. The dual, individually functioning pivot joints worked perfectly in the scale model of the assembler. All that remained of that job was to wait for the fabricators to put the full-scale machine together and kick the big baby into action. He'd have to go on scene at the factory when they fired her up, in case there were any problem areas that needed fine-tuning but, essentially, he was ready to take on a new job.

Each stack of papers before him described a project in need of his particular creative genius. Ordinarily he picked work based on what piqued his interest and challenged him. He liked solving mechanical riddles, designing machines to do what no machine had done before, what no one had ever thought a machine might be able to do. This time, however, he was making his choice based on a different criterion.

The project was mildly interesting. It would be a change of pace working on an amusement-park ride based on a natural-disaster theme. The aspect that made this project most appealing, however, was not the change of pace or the challenge of doing something a little different. The most appealing aspect of this project was the location of the job: Orlando, Florida.

Orlando, as in the home of Miss Keeley Owens, Florida.

Referring to the letterhead of the cover letter, he dialed the appropriate company, asked for the appropriate person and agreed to do the job. The start-up date was more than a month away, which suited his needs perfectly. It would take several days to get on the road and three days to drive to Florida. That would give him three weeks to get to know Keeley in her natural habitat.

After returning home from Vegas, he'd held off calling Keeley until he knew the boyfriend had been back in Orlando a few days. He'd broached the subject of the boyfriend cautiously, trying to make the inquiry seem spontaneous and casual. His heart had skipped a beat when she'd told him Troy had come to the store she managed, but she'd made it clear there would be no reconciliation.

And she was still living alone in that house with the guest room just waiting for a guest.

THE LITTLE GIRL'S FOREHEAD furrowed with lines of concentration. "I didn't know there were girl clowns."

"Sure there are!" Keeley said. "But we don't have big ugly feet like boy clowns." She wiggled her toes for emphasis.

"Those are silly shoes," the child said with a giggle.

Keeley had tried classic clown "big" shoes and found them cumbersome, so she'd made sandals with big plastic flowers that appeared to be growing from between her big toe and the one next to it part of her clown suit. Her toenails were painted hot pink with white dots. "Oh, thank you," she said and then, getting back to business, she asked, "What kind of balloon do you want?"

"Can you make a bunny? I like bunnies."

"I can tell you do," Keeley replied as she began sculpting two balloons into a rabbit. "Do you know how?"

The child shook her head solemnly.

"Because you have a bunny on your dress."

The girl looked down at the appliqué on the yoke of her denim jumper and grinned, then turned her attention back to Keeley, watching intently as Keeley twisted the rabbit's ears into place.

"Here you go, sweetie," Keeley said, passing the balloon sculpture to the child with a hopping motion of her arm. "Here's your bunny." Her heart turned to mush as the little girl flashed her a bashful grin and very politely thanked her for the balloon.

Your clock isn't ticking that fast, she told herself, as she always did when she saw a child and yearned for one of her own. But, as always, the instinctive longing overpowered logic, and telling herself that she had plenty of fertile years ahead of her did nothing to assuage her desire.

Ignoring the yearning, she clapped her hands to get the attention of the children and said, "Does everyone have a balloon now?"

"I'll take another one," said a precocious boy with a mischievous glint in his eye.

"If everyone has a balloon, then it's time to sing 'Happy Birthday' to Ashley. Let's go." She shooed the dozen children to the table where Ashley's mother was waiting to light the candles on a decorated cake, and Mildred, Keeley's next door neighbor, was standing by with a camera, ready to capture the magic of her granddaughter's sixth birthday.

Once the singing was over and Ashley's mother was pouring punch, Keeley went to the kitchen with Mildred to get the ice-cream clowns—single-scoop cones that had been inverted onto a cookie base so that the ice cream formed a head wearing the pointed sugar-cone "hat." Mildred had made the cones, and Keeley had piped on icing facial features, neck ruffles and hat rims before the party.

"These are just precious," Mildred said as they moved the clowns onto paper party plates. "It's so sweet of you to help out with the party. Gracious, Ashley's the only kid in kindergarten to have a real clown."

"It's the least I can do after your husband mowed my lawn."

"It was good for Al. It gave him some extra exercise and got him out of the house," Mildred said. "I have to keep him busy or he's underfoot all day."

"This was good practice for me," Keeley said. "It's been more than a year since I did a party."

"It's made the party so much easier for Barb," Mildred said. Craning her neck, she stole a peep at her daughter-in-law. "I don't know how that girl does it— a six-year-old, a job and now another baby on the way."

Keeley didn't have to crane her neck to observe the festivities from where she was standing. The children were loud, squirmy and altogether wonderful. And Barb, now cutting the cake, was gloriously pregnant. Keeley drew in a sharp breath and tried not to covet Barb's full and hectic life with her faithful husband,

and her sweet mother-in-law, and her darling daughter and her round belly. "Barb's cutting the cake," she said, picking up two plates in each hand. "She needs these."

Another hour passed before the presents were unwrapped and the last party guest was out the door. Keeley collected a big hug and thank-you from Ashley and profuse thank-yous from Mildred and Barb before leaving for home. As she drove the two miles from Barb's house, Keeley mulled over her disturbing reaction to the children and Barb's pregnancy and decided that the uncharacteristic reaction—she was not a petty person by nature, and she wasn't normally envious of other women—must be a side effect of ending the long-standing relationship with Troy. No matter how confident she was about her decision to call off the ceremony in Vegas, she was also aware that breaking up with Troy had put her prospects of marriage and children on hold, relegating them to a remote, fuzzy area of her future. Consciously, she had made an effort not to dwell on the idea, but apparently her subconscious had been actively churning that particular ramification of her breakup with Troy on its own.

As she approached her house, she noticed a pickup truck with a fully loaded bed parked at the curb and wondered idly whose it was. But it wasn't until she'd turned onto the driveway that she saw a man sitting on the porch steps. He rose, and as his huge frame unfolded to extraordinary height, there was no mistaking the identity of her unexpected visitor.

Digby. What was Digby Barnes doing on her doorstep? Even as the question formed in her mind, her body was reacting to his presence; her heart beat a bit faster, her blood ran a bit hotter, her cheeks warmed with a flush of excitement that threatened to melt the clown white she was wearing.

Clown white! Oh, why, why, *why* did Digby Barnes always choose the most absurd moments of her life to show up?

And what was he doing here anyway?

She forced herself to concentrate on parking the car and then walking as normally—as normally as a clown could be expected to act—to the front of the house. Digby didn't bother to hide his incredulity or his amusement at catching her in clown gear.

His eyes sparkled with affection. On another man's face, his grin might have been categorized as "dumb," but on Digby, it was appealing, softening harshness into blatant virility. "Does this...*attire*...mean you're happy to see me?"

She hadn't fully realized, until he said the words, how much she'd missed him. Before she could temper that reaction with logic, she quickened her own step as Digby came toward her in long strides. Seconds later she was in Digby's arms, her feet off the ground as Digby hugged her. "You're going to get makeup on—" she warned, but Digby obviously wasn't concerned about white smudges, because he only hugged her tighter. His mouth found hers with unerring instinct and he kissed her with the intensity of a man who'd been missing a woman too long—who'd been missing *this particular* woman too long.

They might have gone on kissing for hours if something hadn't nudged at Keeley's bare ankle. The startling contact was accompanied by a whine. Laughing,

Digby lowered her until her feet were on the ground. "Damned dog!"

"Is he with you?" Keeley asked. She knelt to pet the fuzzy mutt, a terrier mix with a red bandanna tied around his neck. "What's his name?"

"Chester," Digby replied. "He's your housewarming gift."

"My what?"

"You said you wanted a dog."

"Yes, but...a puppy."

"Puppies are too much trouble," Digby said. "This one's already housebroken. And he likes you."

"I suspect that this little goldbricker would like anyone who paid attention to him," Keeley said of the dog who had just sat down on her foot and was pressing his neck against her hand as she scratched his neck.

"Scratch my neck like that, and I'll roll my eyes back up in my head, too," Digby said.

Keeley looked up to comment and giggled when she saw Digby's face. "You're wearing almost as much makeup as I am." Scooping the dog into her arms, she rose. "Come on in the house and I'll help you clean that off."

"I didn't think you did the clown thing anymore," he said as they walked.

"I haven't in a while. I was doing my neighbor a favor. It was her granddaughter's birthday."

"That was nice of you."

"It was the least I could do. Mildred has been a big help with the house, and Al mowed my lawn because I don't have a lawn mower yet. Anyway, it was good practice. I've been thinking about moonlighting on my days off so I can set up a furniture fund." She fished

her keys from the pocket of the clown shorts and unlocked the front door.

Reality hit as they entered the house. As miscast as
he seemed in the role, up to the moment he passed over
her threshold, Digby had been something of a fantasy
figure rescuing her; taking her out to a show; making
long, sweet love to her; showing up unexpectedly
when she was feeling lonely and lost. But the surprise
of his arrival had worn off enough now for her to respond logically as well as emotionally. Inside her
home, though he still seemed larger than life in the
small living room, Digby Barnes was no fantasy figure.

He was a man, an imposing male presence. Flesh-
and-blood. Solid and virile. A man she scarcely knew,
and yet...a man with whom she'd shared a night of intimacy. Though she quickly resolved to set that
thought aside, she could not escape the awareness of
their history of intimacy. He'd shared some of the most
tumultuous moments of her life, and she could not
simply will that knowledge out of her mind.

"This is nice," Digby commented, giving the room a
once-over.

"I still have a lot of work to do," Keeley said. She'd
added a love seat and an end table to the rocking chair
and small entertainment center, but the walls and ta-
bletops were still bare, and the room still lacked the
warmth and personality she hoped eventually to create
for it. "I'll...uh—" She gestured toward her face and
exhaled heavily. "It shouldn't take me long."

He cupped her elbow. "Keeley."

She looked up at him, meeting his gaze. Unless she
did something to stop it, she realized, he was going to

kiss her again. Taking a step back, she looked down at the dog. "Is he really housebroken?"

"Traveled all the way from Indiana without a single accident."

"Good. But—it probably wouldn't hurt to keep an eye on him anyway."

"I'll keep an eye on him," Digby said.

"Just make yourself at home. There's juice in the refrigerator if you're thirsty." Without waiting for a reaction, she retreated to the bathroom.

Digby went to the love seat and sat down. Chester trailed after him and immediately put his chin on Digby's knee. "Good boy," Digby said, patting the dog on the head. "You really charmed her."

It was risky, of course, letting her have Chester, but if things went the way he suspected they might, he wasn't likely to lose touch with him. Because he didn't plan on losing touch with Keeley Owens anytime soon.

"You've got to keep up the charm, old boy," he told the dog. "I'm counting on you." Chester whimpered and nudged Digby's hand. Digby scratched him behind the ears and, leaning over, said confidentially, "This whole gig depends on it. We can't have her kicking either one of us out, now, can we?"

She was out of the room a long time. Or maybe it just seemed that way because, after waiting so long and driving so far to see her again, he was impatient to spend some time with her.

Finally, she emerged from the back of the house. The clown face was gone, her hair was fluffed and brushed and she had changed into khaki shorts, a rain-forest-motif camp shirt and sandals that weren't sprouting flowers. She looked as good as she had the night she'd stepped into his room. And her smile was almost as timid.

"This should take care of those smudges," she said, offering him a disposable cloth.

Instead of taking it, he rose and bent over slightly, thrusting his face in her direction. "What is that?" he asked as she began dabbing near his mouth.

"A makeup-remover pad."

"It's soothing."

"That's the aloe in it."

It's you, touching me, Digby thought.

All too soon, she gave his cheek a playful tap. "All done."

She turned and disappeared into the adjacent room. Digby followed and stepped into the breakfast nook off the kitchen in time to see her deposit the cloth in a trash pail hidden away in the cabinet under the sink.

Digby looked around the room. Touches of color were sprinkled throughout the room—sunflower magnets on the ancient refrigerator, African violets on the windowsill, sunflower-print seat cushions on the ladder-back chairs. "You've been busy," he said. "This is nice."

"I've only just begun," she answered. "I knew what I wanted in here, so it was just a matter of comparing prices. The rest of the house isn't this together."

Digby flashed her his most charming smile. "How's your guest room?"

"Empty," she answered firmly.

"Excellent. There'll be plenty of room for my stuff until I find a place of my own."

"A place of your own? In Orlando?"

Digby nodded. "I finished up a gizmo last week, and

now I have to find a new gizmo to tinker with. I figured I might as well drum up work here as anywhere else. It's cold enough to freeze the balls off a brass monkey up north."

"Drum up work." Keeley was beginning to feel a little uncomfortable. "So you're...unemployed?"

"Unemployed is a harsh way of putting it. I prefer 'between projects.'"

Keeley frowned. She was beginning to fear that her rescuing knight was wearing tarnished armor. Troy, for all his live-for-the-moment recklessness, had kept a steady job. "You're...'*between projects*,' and so you just decided to move to a strange city?"

"I've never thought of Orlando as strange."

"Orlando *isn't* strange," Keeley said. Though she suspected that he was deliberately misunderstanding, she explained, "I meant strange to you. Unfamiliar. Didn't you say you'd never been here?"

He dismissed her point with a shrug of his shoulders. "Why go to all the trouble to move if you're not going to see new things and meet new people?" He gave her a sizzling look. "Or get to know a certain someone a lot better."

Keeley fought the fluttery reaction to the sensuality smoldering in his eyes. "I can't believe you'd pick up and move somewhere with no job, and—"

He waved away her incredulity. "It's no big deal. I'm used to looking around for work. I've learned to travel light. I'm sure everything will fit perfectly in your guest room until I find a place that doesn't require a long-term lease."

That did it! Any man so flaky he couldn't even commit to signing a lease was bound to be trouble! No matter how nice he'd been to her.

She drew in a ragged breath. *Or how brown his eyes were.* "This is a bit awkward," she said. "Obviously you planned to stay here—"

"Only until I find a place of my own," he said. "A couple of weeks, tops."

"You can't possibly stay here," she said bluntly. "When I said the guest room is empty, I meant it. Literally, it's empty. There's not even a bed."

He grinned sensually. "That's not a problem. I don't mind sharing."

Keeley scowled. *Why was it that the harder she tried not to think about the night they'd spent together, the more detailed her recollections became?* "You're taking too much for granted," she said. "Just because we—"

"Slept together?" he taunted.

"That doesn't give you the right to show up unannounced and move your stuff into my guest room and expect to share my bed," Keeley snapped.

He tucked a strand of hair behind her ear and let his hand linger while he adored her face with his eyes. "You can't blame a guy for wanting more of a good thing."

Trying—unsuccessfully—to ignore the shivers of delight set off by the subtle pressure of his fingers in her hair, his palm cradling her ear, Keeley brushed his hand aside. "It doesn't work that way, Digby. Not with me."

He gave a sniff of frustration. "I wasn't planning on tying you to the bedposts and plundering you, you know." One side of his mouth lifted in a sexy grin. "As appealing as that prospect might be."

His humor threw the situation into perspective, and Keeley felt foolish for having been so brusque. He'd never given her any reason to believe he would force himself on her. Still, she couldn't allow him to barge into her house unannounced—with a dog, no less—and take over her life. Or her bed. "You wouldn't *fit* in my bed," she said, answering humor with humor. "It's a twin."

"I'm sure we could work something out," he said. Noting her censuring glare, he quickly added, "If and when you decide the time is right, that is. For now, I'll roll out my sleeping bag in the guest room."

"You can't sleep on the floor!"

"An old Boy Scout like me? Sure I can."

"Digby, you can't stay here. Period." She took a breath and then added emphatically, "Exclamation point!"

He pouted, looking despite his size, much like a mischievous boy intent on getting his way. "You're not going to make me go to a hotel, are you? They're so...cold and impersonal."

And expensive, Keeley thought. Especially for someone unemployed. Frowning, she said resolutely, "I guess I owe you a rescue."

Digby's triumphant smile came too readily. "I'll start unloading the truck."

10

"DON'T UNLOAD anything yet," Keeley said. "If—and it's still a big if—I let you stay here, we need to talk first."

"Fair enough," he said. "Do you mind if I make a pit stop first? I haven't taken a break since noon."

"It's at the end of the hall," she said. "I'll...uh, be in the living room."

She dropped onto the love seat with a weary sigh. Chester, who'd been sleeping in the middle of the floor, roused, walked over to put his chin on her knee. Keeley scratched him behind the ears. "I should have *easy* stamped across my forehead," she grumbled.

The terrier regarded her with soulful eyes, as though he understood her every word. "I must have rocks in my head even to consider letting him stay here!"

Chester whimpered sympathetically. "Sorry, boy," Keeley said. "You're a nice doggie. You're not the problem. It's that big galoot who brought you here."

Chester whimpered again and nuzzled his chin closer against her knee. Keeley laughed softly. "All right, you little goldbricker. Come on up." She patted her lap and he was in it instantly, immediately curling and cuddling as though he'd been doing so since puppyhood. Idly massaging the dog's ears, Keeley sighed. *That nice...big...sexy galoot.*

What did she know about him, really? The man was

drifting through life with no more direction than a feather in the wind, going wherever he could catch a flight, flitting from job to job with no thought of tomorrow, doing whatever occurred to him at the moment, without regard—

"You two seem to be getting on well," Digby observed, entering the room from the hallway.

"It's a fairly straightforward relationship," Keeley said, looking with fondness at the scruffy little mutt. "I pet him, and he lets me." She was, in fact, kneading the side of the dog's neck between his ear and collar. As if on cue, the dog exhaled a sigh worthy of a Victorian virgin.

Smiling, Keeley glanced up at Digby, intending to ask where he'd gotten Chester. But her breath caught in her throat when she saw him gazing at her, a smile on his face. How had she ever thought that face severe? It wasn't severe at all. There was too much warmth in the eyes, too much sincerity in the smile, too much passion in the upward curves of his mouth. She could not look at his broad shoulders, wide chest and strong arms without remembering reassuring hugs, could not see his lips without recalling the press of heated kisses on flushed skin, could not look at his huge hands without feeling shivers of delight raised by skillful caresses.

"He seems content with the new arrangement," he said, closing the distance between them in two long strides to take a seat beside her, bringing the scent of male cologne with him to tantalize her.

"Where did you find him?" Keeley asked, willing her reaction to Digby aside.

"At the pound." He grinned devilishly. "I rescued him." *Two years ago, when he was a puppy.*

"That figures."

"What can I say? It's a way of life." He reached out to pat the dog's head, meeting Keeley's gaze as his fingers brushed against hers. Though the contact was accidental, he seized the opportunity to make the most of it by intentionally tracing his thumb over the back of her hand.

Her eyes narrowed as she tried not to react to his touch. *Good.* He didn't want denying the chemistry between them to be easy for her.

"So what did you want to talk about?" he asked.

"You," she said, subtly moving her hand out of his reach. "Us. Digby, if you're going to stay here, we need to talk about what happened in Vegas."

Digby pulled his hand into his lap. Why women had to make something complicated out of the simplest things was a mystery to him. They'd connected—that's what had happened in Vegas.

"We met under extraordinary circumstances," she continued.

"That's putting it mildly."

"I was in a bad situation."

"You were doing high kicks in the middle of the highway wearing a wedding dress."

She scowled displeasure. "I wasn't just angry. I was also hurt and confused and in a state of emotional distress. And you were on vacation, ready for...adventure." She paused to collect her thoughts. "The point is, neither of us was...well, in a normal frame of mind. I was vulnerable, and you were in a generous mood, and under those extraordinary circumstances—"

"The point is," Digby said with an edge of bitterness,

"now that everything is back to normal, you don't think we ought to make love anymore."

Keeley exhaled heavily. "If you stay here, it's going to be with that stipulation. I just ended a relationship with a man who couldn't make commitments—at least not big ones. The ones that count. I'm not going to make the same mistake again."

"You're comparing apples and oranges, Keeley. I'm not Troy. I'm not anything like him."

"You can't just pack up and move cross-country with no job and show up on my doorstep unannounced—with a *dog*, no less—wanting to stay in my guest room until God knows when, and expect me to think of you as the prince of responsibility," Keeley said.

Digby silently counted to ten to control his temper before answering. There was plenty he could tell her. *Plenty.* But he refused to defend himself. Until Keeley Owens was able to accept him for who he was, judging him on the merit of his actions rather than comparing him to a man who'd let her down, no amount of argument would win him the kind of respect he wanted from her. So instead of telling her about D. B. Innovations or whipping out his portfolio to impress her, he said softly, "You're confusing responsibility with conformity, Keeley. Troy couldn't handle responsibility. I can handle responsibility. I just don't always feel like coloring inside the lines."

Keeley digested that comment thoughtfully before replying, "You can play with words all you want, Digby. The bottom line is, I'm not twenty years old anymore. I had enough spontaneity with Troy to last a lifetime. Now I'm ready for grown-up things."

"Like children," Digby said.

"Yes. I want children. I haven't made any secret of that. But I want the whole package. You said you don't always feel like coloring inside the lines. Well, I want to. I don't want to raise children alone. I want a father who's going to be as involved in raising our children as I am." She paused. "I know what it's like to grow up without a father, wishing for one, knowing that he couldn't live up to the responsibility, wondering why he's not—"

She choked back a lump of emotion. Her pain was almost palpable, and Digby knew he had glimpsed a part of her she seldom uncovered: Keeley, the fatherless child, the abandoned daughter, set aside by the father who wasn't man enough to be a father.

"So," she continued brusquely, "while I don't mind returning your kindness in Vegas, it's going to be friend-to-friend, not lover-to-lover."

"No time to waste on a rolling stone?"

She met his gaze evenly. "I don't have time to invest in a relationship that would lead straight to limbo."

Digby couldn't conceal the edge in his voice. "And you are so sure that's where we'd be headed?"

"You don't even make plane reservations!"

"Since when is that a character flaw?" He added an epithet that expressed his frustration over her attitude.

The word hung in the air for a long, awkward moment before Keeley offered him a conciliatory smile. "It wouldn't be—in a friend."

Digby recognized her comment for the ultimatum it was: he was welcome to stay as her friend, but not as her lover. He didn't like it, but it was the best he was going to get.

For now.

He traced the curve of the curl he'd tucked behind her ear earlier, and she turned her head, facing him.

Peering into her eyes intently, he asked, "Do you know how much I'd like to make love to you right this minute?"

She poised her mouth to speak but then, as though she'd changed her mind, she looked away. Digby felt like heaving a sigh of relief, but held it in. Having found out what he'd wanted to know, he decided to play it cool.

He stood up. "If that's not an option, then I guess I might as well go to plan B."

She took the bait. "Plan B?"

"Unload the truck." He started to the door.

"Digby?"

He stopped, turned, lifted an eyebrow.

"You understand the conditions if you stay here?" she asked.

"I understand." Boy, did he understand. He understood so well he ached.

As he reached for the knob, Chester sprang from Keeley's lap and made a dash for the door. Reaching it just as Digby closed it, he whimpered, sniffed along the bottom of the door and then plopped down, chin on paws, to wait.

Keeley leaned her head against the back of the love seat and groaned. What had she done?

"MAYBE I CAN HELP YOU," Digby said.

Keeley stopped tucking the bottom sheet around the mattress of the bed that pulled out of the love seat, but didn't look up. "I'm almost done."

It was bad enough having him *watch* her make the bed in which he'd be sleeping; she didn't think she could endure any chummy teamwork where they each took a corner. Not after he'd made it so clear that he would prefer to be sleeping with her.

Although the subject hadn't come up again, the few hours of camaraderie, light conversation and preparing a simple meal together since that little chat were more than enough to convince her that sharing a house the size of hers with a man the size of Digby Barnes was going to give new meaning to the word *share*. He was going to be underfoot, under elbow, over the shoulder, in the bathtub and across the table—grinning and smiling, scowling and frowning, cocking his eyebrow in that acerbic way he so succinctly expressed skepticism. There wasn't going to be a moment Digby was anywhere, doing anything, in her house that she would be unaware that he was one hundred percent male.

"I didn't mean with the bed," Digby said, mentally giving himself a point for using the word *bed*. Phase two of plan B was to keep Keeley thinking about possibilities without seeming to be doing so deliberately. The fact that she'd been avoiding looking at him while making the bed was a hopeful sign. "I meant with the right man."

That made her look up. "The right man?"

"I was just thinking—it's not easy for a single woman to meet men. I could escort you around, take you places you couldn't—or rather, wouldn't—go alone."

"Like where?"

He shrugged his shoulders. "Sports bars, maybe.

Lots of single men go to sports bars, especially for big games."

"You want to help me meet men? By taking me to sports bars?"

"Not just *men*. Professional men." *Mr. Responsibility.* "The future father of your children. I could strike up conversations, help you screen the prospects." Phase two of plan B also included keeping track of any potential competition. "We might find you a lawyer. Or a chiropractor."

"A chiropractor?"

"Very secure. Chiropractic is the medicine of the future. No drugs. And lots of...hands on. Chiropractors probably make great lovers. All those machines—"

"Digby!" Her face was red as fire.

Digby grinned affably. "What do you think of the idea?"

"You don't want to know what I think!" Keeley said. She attacked the bottom edge of the blanket and crammed it under the thin mattress.

Digby feigned obliviousness. "Did I say something wrong?"

Scowling, she sniffed indignantly. Digby watched her breasts bulge against her shirt as she crossed her arms in front of her. She'd never looked sexier. Straining to keep a straight face, he shrugged. "You said you wanted to be friends, and finding a responsible guy seems to be important to you. I thought...I was just trying to—"

"Well, just quit trying, okay? You don't have to *rescue* me from spinsterhood, you know! I'm not that desperate for a man."

"Sorry," he said. "I thought—"

"Well, don't think!" Having finished tucking in the bottom of the blanket, she moved to the head of the bed and yanked it straight.

"Ever?" he teased, impulsively stretching out on the bed atop the blanket and crossing one ankle over the other.

Keeley finished working the pillow into a pillowcase, plumped it and tossed it at him, hitting him squarely in the face. Laughing, he shoved it under his head and, tucking his palms beneath his nape, snuggled into the pillow's feathery depths. With his ankles crossed and his elbows spread, he looked totally at ease. Totally confident.

Totally desirable. Keeley tried not to notice, but the effort was futile. The blatantly obvious truth simply couldn't be ignored. The man was an Adonis.

She should have let him sleep on the floor in the guest room instead of telling him about the foldout bed. But she knew he would be more comfortable on a thin mattress a foot off the floor than in a sleeping bag *on* the floor, so she'd insisted on making the bed.

He pushed up on one elbow. "Want to watch a movie?"

"It's a little late," she said. *And the bed's already made.*

"Aw, come on," he cajoled. "Humor me. I drove a long way today. I need to unwind. Let's watch something funny."

She sighed resignedly and walked over to the entertainment center. Kneeling in front of the shelved videotapes, she read titles aloud until he said, "I've heard that one's good."

"It's one of my favorites," she said, taking the tape from the shelf. "I haven't watched this in ages." She put it in the VCR, and turned around. Digby had taken off his shoes and was propped up against the throw pillows from the love seat.

"You look comfortable," she commented. Comfortable—and sexy as a poster hunk.

"Care to join me?" he asked with a naughty grin.

"I wouldn't want to crowd you." She'd joked that he wouldn't fit in her single bed, but there had been truth in the jest. He more than adequately filled the foldout bed.

"I could move over," he said, doing so as he spoke. But when he patted the space next to him, Chester, who'd been lying contentedly on the floor, leaped up to accept what he perceived as an invitation. A bundle of enthusiasm, he licked Digby in the face and then stretched out beside him, rolling onto his back. Pressing his head against Digby's ribs, he whimpered for attention.

"And you thought you were going to be lonely," Keeley said with smug triumph. He'd been pushing the rules, and she'd been ready to push them with him. She settled into the rocker, kicked off her slippers and propped her feet on the edge of the bed.

"Nice pedicure," Digby said as he idly kneaded the dog's ears.

Keeley giggled and wiggled her toes. "Dots are all the rage among clowns."

He grabbed the foot closest to his hand and gave it a playful squeeze. "Girl clowns."

Digby had surprised her. She hadn't realized how close she was to him, how easy it would be for him to touch her. It had not occurred to her that he might want to touch her foot that way, nor had the possibility crossed her mind that a playful tweak of his bear-paw hand could seem so intimate. Had it seemed that way to him? she wondered. Had he meant it to be, or was it the simple, spontaneous gesture it appeared to be? Was the intimacy in her perception, his intent or both?

If he had intimacy in mind, he did a masterful job of hiding it. With the orchestral theme music of the movie providing a backdrop, she searched his face for a clue to what he was thinking or feeling.

Their eyes met. Digby smiled warmly and asked, "You wouldn't happen to have any popcorn, would you?"

11

DIGBY STOLE a peep at Keeley over the top of the sports section of the morning paper. Dressed in lightweight slacks and an oxford shirt with the long sleeves rolled up to her elbows, she was leaning negligently against the jamb of the door that led into the living room from the kitchen. Though it was midmorning, she was still nursing her first mug of coffee, holding it distractedly while she stared at the wall behind the love seat.

"Did that love seat do something to you?" Digby asked.

"Hmm?" Keeley responded absently.

"The way you're scowling at it, I thought maybe you were getting ready to go after it with an ax."

"I was looking at the wall," she said. "It needs something."

Digby set the paper aside and walked over to her. Stopping behind her, he leaned forward until his chin rested on her shoulder, trying to evaluate the wall from her perspective. Was his hand curving around her waist the innocent gesture it seemed?

"You're right," he said. "It needs something." *And you smell good.* He could so easily have kissed that sweet little neck mere inches from his mouth. "What'd you have in mind?"

"Something...dramatic," she said.

"A painting?" Though he'd lifted his chin, he kept his hands on her shoulders.

"I don't know. I don't want to stick something up there just to have something on the wall. Some kind of sculpture might work. Something contemporary, with metals and lots of open space in the design." She sighed. "Of course, I'd have to clown every day off from now to the middle of the next century to pay for the kind I'm thinking about."

"Why don't you try making something yourself?"

Turning, she looked at Digby as though he'd suggested she try a little amateur brain surgery. "Oh, sure. I'll see if Al has an old rake and ask Mildred to clean out her cooking-utensil drawer."

"Sounds like a good place to start."

"Get a grip on reality!" Keeley said. "Art has to...say something. I made a C in fifth-grade art because I couldn't make something out of corks and paper clips. I don't even remember what I was supposed to be making."

"Maybe you had a lousy art teacher."

"There was nothing wrong with *her*," Keeley said. "I was the one who couldn't come up with anything artistic."

"Art teachers should inspire creativity, not scare it out of you."

Rolling her eyes in exasperation, she said, "She was a lousy teacher. I was a lousy student. Does it matter? Either way, the idea of my making a wall sculpture is ludicrous."

He extended his arms, holding his hands up with his thumbs touching, "framing" the wall like a photographer composing a shot. "You'll never know what you might have come up with if you don't at least try."

"Trust me, I know," Keeley assured him. "I tried fabric painting on a T-shirt once."

Digby dropped his arms and, with an exaggerated frown, shook his head at her. "Where's your sense of adventure? Your natural urge to express yourself?"

"My chrysanthemum turned out looking like an overcooked head of cauliflower!"

"You've got a day off. Let's see what we can come up with," he cajoled.

"We?"

Digby tweaked the tip of her nose with his forefinger. "I'll help you. Tinkering is my life's work, remember?"

"I couldn't make a wall sculpture if Michelangelo came back from the grave to act as a consultant!"

"You don't know who you're dealing with, lady. By the time we're finished with your wall, Michelangelo is going to look like a rank amateur."

"I'll alert the Vatican. They'll probably want us to revamp the Sistine Chapel for them."

"We have nothing to lose but a little time and a few bucks. At the very least we'll have some fun."

"There's more to life than fun," she said, thinking that, for a man without a steady job, he was awfully quick to dismiss a few bucks. Especially her bucks. "Don't you have something you need to be doing today?" *Like hunting for a job? Or an apartment?* She had no idea how much progress he'd made in either quest. He'd gone out—somewhere—several times while she was at work, but she didn't know where he'd gone. He'd mentioned an appointment at one of the movie parks, but she wasn't sure which one or what kind of job he'd gone to discuss. And he'd gotten a call from some kind of leasing agent, which she assumed concerned an apartment he'd either looked at or called about, but he hadn't shared any details with her.

Oddly, though logic would dictate the opposite, the longer he stayed, the more difficult it was for her to think of him as a freeloader. He was too likable for such an unflattering label—amiable, quick to pitch in and help with any job that needed doing, easy to talk to and, even more surprising, easy to be with when neither felt the urge to talk. He'd been in her house less than a week, and his presence was as comfortable as the tattered terry slippers she couldn't make herself discard.

Except for the sex thing, of course.

Digby had been a perfect gentleman, neither mentioning their previous experience nor attempting to initiate a new one, but the fact remained that they'd had sex and they were attracted to each other. Whether tossing a salad, folding freshly laundered towels or walking the dog, the awareness was always there between them. There were times when Keeley almost wished—

"You're right," he said. "There *is* something I desperately need to do today."

Keeley fought back the traitorous disappointment she felt. Trying to make a wall sculpture was a fool's mission, but the idea of doing something frivolous and unanticipated on her day off appealed to her—more than she liked to admit, especially since she'd sworn off men who lived moment to moment.

Her heart soared when Digby's face broke into a grin

and he said, "I have to take you out and show you how to have a little fun."

Refusing to give him the satisfaction of an enthusiastic capitulation, Keeley looked down at her terry slippers and grumbled, "I'll put on shoes."

THEY WENT to every thrift store within ten miles. Digby charged through each of them with the intense focus of Sherlock Holmes chasing down a culprit, while Keeley scurried along like a female Watson, suitably befuddled.

"What are we looking for?" she asked in the first store.

"Potential," he said without slowing down.

"Right," she said, following his gaze to a room filled with a hodgepodge collection of mismatched furniture. Most of the pieces were scratched, some missing drawer pulls, some with doors gaping because of broken latches. "And am I supposed to be seeing it here?"

"Not necessarily," he said, "as long as you're open to the possibility of finding it."

After a moment, she asked curiously, "Do you see any?"

Digby shook his head. "Not in this corner."

They moved on. Keeley couldn't see potential anywhere in the store, but Digby ferreted out a length of copper tubing, which he insisted fairly vibrated with it. As they made their way to the check out counter, slowly zigzagging between the shelves laden with eclectic discards, a tall, slender V-shaped vase—or was it a glass?—captured Keeley's eye. She stopped to gaze at it nostalgically. "This reminds me—"

"Of your first roses?" Digby asked.

Embarrassed, Keeley confessed, "No one's ever sent me roses." She sighed. "Roses weren't Troy's style."

"What does this remind you of, then?"

"There was a soda fountain in the drugstore in my hometown. They used to have a lot of glasses like this."

"Buy it."

Tempted, Keeley picked up the vase and examined it. "It's chipped on the base."

She placed it back on the shelf, but Digby picked it up and tucked it under his arm. "You never know."

"It's chipped, Digby."

"It's twenty-five cents," he replied. "There's a quarter's worth of potential in it because of sentimental attachment."

Keeley frowned, and Digby laughed. "If we don't find a way to use it, we'll throw it against a mantel and make a wish."

"I don't have a mantel," she said as he marched to the checkout counter.

"We'll improvise," he said. "I'm sure you can find some surface in your house hard enough to shatter glass."

They acquired a china rosebud at the next store. After the incident with the vase, Keeley refrained from pointing out that the stem was missing and silently vowed not to admire anything else for fear Digby would insist she buy it.

In the furniture section, Digby lingered next to a laminate-top dining table with black pole legs for a few moments, apparently searching for some illusive promise of potential. Much to Keeley's relief, he walked on after examining the brittle plastic cushions of the matching chairs. But seconds later, his pace quickened until, finally, he stopped next to a dilapidated metal patio set.

"This is incredible," he said after looking at the table from every angle.

"No argument there," Keeley said. Though the table and two chairs must have been lovely at one time, they were in hopeless disrepair, the original white paint reduced to ghostly pale patches. One of the table legs was badly misshapen, the once-graceful, even artful, curves of the heavy wire lost in a severe bend that made it kick out and shortened it well over an inch. The tabletop slanted severely and, when barely jostled, the entire thing rocked unsteadily. The chairs were equally battered.

"Don't you see it?" Digby asked, turning his head to look at Keeley as he spoke. "There's an emerging theme."

"Emerging theme?" She shook her head. "I'm sorry. I just don't—"

"Ice cream!" he said. "The vase reminded you of a glass from a soda fountain, and this table and these chairs could have come from an old-fashioned ice-cream parlor."

"Maybe," she allowed, in the interest of fairness. Actually she thought it more likely the set had been sitting on the patio of an abandoned house somewhere. A *long*-abandoned house, judging from the dirt dauber nests and cobwebs.

"I don't see a price," he said, searching for one.

"They're probably embarrassed to accept money for it," she said.

Undaunted, Digby picked up the table. "We'll use that to our advantage. Maybe they'll deal."

"If they offer you any less than five dollars to cart it off, you ought to hold out for more."

"Very funny," he said. "Can you get the chairs, or do I have to make two trips?"

"I'll get them," she said, but she was beginning to wonder if she should be encouraging him.

Digby dickered the price down to four dollars. Keeley reached for her purse, but he waved away the gesture and pulled out his wallet. As he slapped a five-dollar bill on the glass counter, he looked past it, into the enclosed showcase. "Does that lamp work?"

"It should," the cashier said. "This is our deluxe-item case. If it didn't work, it wouldn't be in here." She took the lamp from the case and set it on the counter in front of him. It was the kind with a bulb hidden in the base and a cluster of thin plastic reeds that fell outward in all directions. When the bulb was lit, the light appeared to travel through the reeds and pool at the tips, as though each were an individual bulb.

"I haven't seen one of those in years," Keeley said. "My best friend had one. We called it her firecracker lamp."

"It looks like moonlight to me," Digby cooed sensually into her ear. He kissed her cheek and told the clerk they wanted the lamp.

They returned to Keeley's house after an early lunch. Digby's impatience to get started on their project was evident as he sprang from the driver's side of the pickup's cab and began unloading their purchases. "You take the small stuff inside and I'll meet you on the patio," he told her.

"Frankenstein and his monster," Keeley grumbled,

juggling the various bags as she dug in her handbag for her keys.

"You might want to change into some old clothes," Digby called after her. "It's going to be dirty work for a while."

Dirty work indeed! Keeley thought as she pulled on an old, stretched-out T-shirt. Stained and threadbare, the shirt settled over her with the patina of familiarity, and suddenly she recalled the shirt Digby had loaned her in Vegas, the faded Bulls shirt that had fit her like a minidress. They'd been off on a caper when she'd worn it, too. At least they'd had a practical reason to embark on that one, and a fair chance of success. The odds of making something worth hanging on the wall out of that beat-up old table were somewhere between nil and nonexistent.

When she led Chester out the back door to tether him to the tie out post, Digby was scrubbing the table and chairs with a wire brush. "Where'd the brush come from?" she asked.

"My tool kit," he said. "No self-respecting tinkerer would travel without a wire brush."

"Of course not," Keeley said, her heart swelling with affection for the man she was beginning to know so well; the tinkerer. "So what's next?"

Digby looked at the dripping furniture and frowned. "You can hold them steady while I get the kinks out of the legs."

"You're *never* going to get them back to their original condition," Keeley said.

"They don't have to be perfect. We're going to flatten them anyway."

"I'd ask how we were going to do that, but I probably wouldn't want to know."

"Unless you know someone with a bulldozer, we're going to have to do it the old-fashioned way. Right now, come over here and brace this table while I work on this leg." He had turned the table on its side, with the most misshapen leg on the patio. Sitting cross-legged, Keeley grasped the tabletop and steadied it while Digby wielded pliers and a hammer with the finesse of a surgeon applying scalpels and forceps. She watched him through the openings in the flower-motif cutwork pattern of the tabletop, fascinated by the accuracy of his hands—hands so large they had no right to be graceful—and the skill with which he exerted his considerable strength to apply the exact amount of force needed to shape the metal.

"I hadn't realized the pattern in this top was so delicate," she said. "It must have been stunning when it was new."

Digby stopped working and smiled. "What's this? Is Keeley Owens actually looking beneath the surface?"

"I can see how it might have been pretty once, but I gotta tell you, Digby, I still don't see much future in it."

"Oh ye of little faith," he said, rotating the table to work on the next leg.

It took him about ten minutes to finish the table and another half hour on the chairs. Finally satisfied, he arranged the set as though two people were sitting there then stepped back and "framed" the tableau as he had the wall earlier. He adjusted the chairs slightly, then stepped back again to reevaluate.

"What are you doing?" Keeley asked.

"Getting some perspective on angles." Careful not to

disturb the chairs, he lifted the table up and away, tilting it on its side again. "And now for the fun part."

He raised his right leg and centered his foot on the topmost section of the tabletop, then pressed it forward with a grunt of exertion. After a second or two of resistance, the table collapsed. Digby surveyed the results and rubbed his hands together in glee. "Damn, I'm good!"

He flipped a chair over on its back and looked at Keeley. "I'm going to need your help."

Keeley nodded. "Just tell me what to do."

He pointed to the back of the chair. "Just stand on this and look adorable."

The curved surface rocked as she stepped onto it.

"It might shift when I try to collapse it," he warned as he poised his foot on the corner of the seat. "Be ready to balance yourself. On three. One...two... three!"

Under the force of his giant's foot, the seat yielded, but the chair back bounced up, sending Keeley tumbling backward. Gasping, Digby lunged to catch her, pulling her sideways atop him as he rolled under her to absorb her fall.

After an interval of dead silence, Keeley recovered from the shock of the fall enough to notice other things. Like a warm, hard male pressed against her. A strong male arm beneath her. Expensive male cologne. A heart beating steadily near her ear. "Are you all right?" she asked.

She felt laughter vibrate through him as he folded his arm around her, hugging her. "I couldn't be better."

"You're not hurt?"

"I'm aching," he said, his voice heavy with a sensual undertone. "But not from the fall."

Keeley twisted her head so she could see his face. "So why aren't you kissing me?"

He hesitated before caressing her cheek with his fingertips. His gaze locked with hers. "I lay awake at night thinking about kissing you." His hand slid higher until his fingers wove into her hair and then he closed his hand into a fist around it. "Don't ask me to kiss you and expect me to stop there."

Keeley's entire body tingled and warmed. Her face felt as though it had been set afire. He was right. They couldn't kiss like people on a first date. Not after what had happened between them in Vegas.

And she couldn't give into chemistry—not when he was so wrong for her. She needed a stable, reliable man, not a flaky *tinkerer.* Turning her head with a forlorn sigh, she grumbled, "Damned hormones."

"Yeah," Digby said. "Ditto." Gingerly extracting his arm from beneath her, he rolled away from her and sat up. "I think I'll have myself neutered and move to Tibet to become a monk."

"That would be cheating, wouldn't it?" Keeley asked. "Isn't the whole point of taking vows of celibacy to practice sacrifice and self-control?"

"You do celibate your way, and I'll do it mine," he grumbled. "This celibacy thing wasn't my idea in the first place."

Keeley frowned. Did he think it was any easier for her? Maybe if he got miserable enough, he'd move out.

The thought did little to cheer her.

Jarred from deep thought by an odd, discordant clacking noise, she turned to see Digby standing on the collapsed chair. He balanced himself, then jumped, producing another clack. "Damn!" he growled, looking down at the chair. "I wish I had a sledgehammer."

"I'm surprised you don't have one with you."

"I forgot to pack it." He tipped the second chair on its side. "Are you game to try the same thing again—without the fall this time?"

"I was afraid you'd never ask," she said, stepping onto the chair back.

Digby poised his foot on the rim of the seat. "Ready? On three." But instead of counting, Digby frowned. Finally, he said, "I don't want you to fall again."

"I'm not going to fall."

"That's what you said last time."

"I know what to expect this time."

"You'd better put your arms around my waist, just in case."

"I'll bet you use this technique on every girl you meet," Keeley said, wrapping her arms around him.

"I try," he said, "but up to now, it's only worked on blondes."

Exasperated, Keeley gave him a whack on the butt.

He leered at her and grinned devilishly. "I've never tried that kind of thing, but I like to think of myself as open-minded."

"On three," Keeley said pointedly. "One...two—"

"Three!" Digby said, lunging forward. They wobbled a bit, but stayed on their feet.

"Now what?" Keeley said, eyeing the smashed chair as she stepped way from Digby.

"We start creating," Digby said. He dragged the chairs to the table and placed them on opposite sides, tucking the edge of the flattened seats beneath the tabletop in an approximation of the way they would be

arranged if they weren't smashed flat as lumpy pan-
cakes made by a really bad cook.

He stepped back, "framed" his handiwork and adjusted the angle of one of the chairs, tilting it out
slightly. "What do you think?"

Keeley studied the arrangement with narrowed
eyes. "It looks—" She hesitated a long, pregnant moment, then exhaled dismally before concluding,
"—like something that fell off a truck in rush-hour traffic."

"Ingrate," Digby said, grabbing her hand. He started
walking toward the front yard, pulling her along with
him.

Perplexed, Keeley half ran to keep up with his long
strides until, finally, they reached his truck. Nonchalantly letting go of her hand, he climbed into the truck
bed, unlocked a metal toolbox mounted parallel to the
cab and began sorting through a stack of macho-
looking tools and related paraphernalia. At length he
tossed her a spool of thin wire. "Here. Hold on to this.
We're going to need it."

"We?"

"You're going to help," he informed her. Then, grinning, he added, "Maybe your attitude will improve after you do a little righteous work."

"There's nothing wrong with my attitude," Keeley
grumbled.

Digby grinned devilishly. "Unlike that hot little
body of yours—" he underscored the suggestive comment by eyeing her from head to toe "—your attitude
toward our artistic collaboration leaves much to be desired. There is a blatant lack of enthusiasm on your
end."

"Pardon me if roadkill furniture doesn't send me into a swoon."

When they returned to the patio, Digby again evaluated the arrangement of the flattened metal ensemble, then marked with chalk all the places where the table touched either chair. Next, he wired the three pieces together wherever openings in the metal presented a feasible site, recruiting Keeley's help to poke the wire through the openings from the top or catch it as he fed it back through from underneath.

"Will this skinny wire hold when we try to pick this up?" Keeley asked.

"This wire would hold *you* if I decided to hang you up by your thumbs," he said.

"There's a reassuring thought," she murmured.

He looked up to meet her gaze. "You know I'd never do a thing like that to a nice girl like you." He grinned devilishly. "No matter how cheeky you get."

Keeley sniffed disdainfully and turned her head in a benign snub. Digby dismissed the playful insult with a hearty chuckle.

Despite their bantering—or perhaps, because of it—working with Digby was easy.

Being near him without being *near* him was a different matter. It could have been his size that created the illusion that he was surrounding her, but Keeley suspected that it was more her sensual sensitivity to him. She felt his warmth, smelled his cologne, sensed his strength. She had but to close her eyes and imagine herself back in that hotel room in Vegas to remember what it was like to be with him, recalling his hardness, his gentleness and the intensity of his lovemaking.

The temptation to touch him was strong, almost overwhelming. It would have been easy. One small move in his direction. And she knew, with a woman's intuition, that if she made that small concession, Digby would take her in his embrace. Oh, how she longed to be folded into those strong arms and pressed against that wide chest, to escape the world by taking refuge in the serenity and safety they offered.

A sigh slipped silently from her throat. If only they could hug, and the world would stand still. If only they could kiss, and the moment would freeze with the splendor of it. If only they could make love, and the sweetness of it would transport them into a secret place where nothing existed outside of the feelings they shared. If only nothing mattered except the closeness they could share. If only time didn't go on, today didn't become tomorrow and pragmatic concerns like shared values and common goals were irrelevant. If only basic goodness and sexual chemistry were enough of a foundation for forever.

She took advantage of his preoccupation with his work to study his face, and silently laughed at herself. His strong jaw was set, his forehead crinkled with concentration. Had she really thought this face was severe? It was not severity she'd been looking at, but character.

As if sensing her scrutiny, he tilted his head back and, catching her watching him, he smiled warmly.

What that smile did to her insides was unfair, she decided. As unfair as the rest of life. Life had to be unfair; otherwise, why would a man who seemed so right be so wrong for her?

And why would she have fallen head over heels in love with him?

12

"DO WHAT?" Keeley looked perplexed. *Adorably* perplexed.

"Flick it," Digby said, wrapping his hand around hers and guiding it. "Like this. It's all in the wrist. Splatter the paint across the surface."

She twisted her head to look at his face, and her hair, soft as silk, grazed his cheek. "Isn't the main objective of painting not to splatter?"

"There you go again," Digby teased. "Coloring inside the lines. This is art. You don't want a solid swash of color, you want subtlety."

"Subtlety," Keeley said with a note of rebellious mischief. Moving her hand away from his, she plunged her brush into the small bottle of paint, brought it out with the bristles fully saturated and gave a decisive flick of her wrist. Droplets of cherry-pink paint scattered across the top of the flattened table.

Across the newspaper underneath the table.

Across Keeley's shin and Digby's thigh. Keeley's chin and Digby's cheek. Keeley's breast and Digby's fly. Digby swallowed indignantly and said with strained irony, "By George, I think you've got it!"

Keeley shrugged, and said sweetly, "I flicked. It splattered."

Digby clenched his jaw with enough force to dent nails. No one appearing that innocent could possibly be so. With one side of his mouth turned down in a semifrown, he rubbed a spot of paint from Keeley's cheek with his forefinger and smeared it haphazardly across the table, passing his fingertip through several splotches of red along the way.

"You smeared it!" Keeley said.

Digby's eyebrows flew up. "Is that concern I hear in your voice?" he asked. "Don't tell me you're starting to *care* about our project."

"I...it seems silly to mess it up."

"But that's the whole point. We're going to mess it up. As soon as the other colors are splattered on, we're going to smear them all around and wipe most of the paint off."

"Oh," she said. "In that case—" She scraped a smudge from his cheek and wiped her finger on the tabletop.

Digby countered by lethargically mopping the long splotch from her shin and similarly applying it to the table. Then he looked at her, at the paint on his thigh and back at her, daring her.

She took the dare, pressing into his muscle with much more pressure than necessary and deliberately letting her fingertips linger on his thigh before finally moving her hand away. It was heaven having her touch him.

It was also exquisite torture. He punished her by settling his gaze on the bright spot of hot pink on her shirt above her breast, and said, "Too bad about your shirt."

She countered by staring at the fly of his pants. "Too bad about your shorts."

After a stalemated silence, Digby shrugged. "Let's

get the other colors on before this one dries too much to blend well."

Keeley picked up another bottle of paint. "How'd you learn so much about art?" she asked as she tried to twist open the lid. After a pilgrimage to the craft department of the local discount store, Digby had sprayed the metal pieces with a base coat of bronze metallic paint. They'd taken a break while it dried, and now they were adding the highlight colors Keeley had selected.

"My mom used to enroll me in art classes in the summer. I think she was afraid I'd inherited my father's left-brainedness."

"What does your father do with his left brain?"

"He designs automobile exhaust systems."

"My dad wanted to be an actor," Keeley said, still struggling with the bottle lid. "When I was a little girl, I used to fantasize that he'd become a big movie star and ask me to visit him in his Hollywood mansion."

"Here," Digby said, reaching for the bottle, "let me have that." The lid yielded on his first attempt. He removed it and gave the paint back to Keeley.

"Are your parents still married?" she asked almost wistfully as she dipped her brush in the paint.

"Thirty-five years last April."

"That's sweet."

"Better or worse, richer or poorer, in sickness and in health," he said. "They went through a lot together, good and bad, but they always weathered it."

"You were lucky to have both of them," Keeley said.

Digby nodded. "Yes. They're great parents. I guess that's why I haven't gotten married yet. I've been waiting for a woman I wouldn't mind spending that many years with, a woman who would be willing to work at making a marriage work instead of bailing out at the first sign of trouble." He paused briefly. "Relationships like that start with acceptance."

He could tell Keeley was thinking about what he'd said when she turned her head, paying particular attention to the brush as she jiggled the tip in the paint before splattering teal across the tabletop.

"Acceptance?" she asked without looking up.

"Nobody's perfect," he said, "and no two people are alike. The secret to a long-term partnership is accepting your partner for who and what he—or she—is, and then finding a way to make your combined strengths and weaknesses complement each other."

He was talking about them, Keeley realized. About her refusal to accept the fact that he was a flake. Well, some things just weren't acceptable. "Do we need more of this, or should I go to the Arctic white?" she asked, hoping to steer the subject into more comfortable territory.

"Use lots of teal," he said. "On the chairs, too. It'll give a verdigris undertone to the bronze."

"Just what I've always wanted," Keeley mumbled. "A verdigris undertone."

"Could you muster just a little enthusiasm for this project?" Digby asked exasperatedly.

She dipped the brush and flicked paint several times. "There! How's that for enthusiasm?"

"Better," he said. "Now the white. Just a touch."

"*Arctic* white," Keeley said. "We couldn't use just any ordinary old white with verdigris. Especially not on a Digby Barnes original."

"A Barnes-Owens original," he corrected.

"Oh, no. This...*creation* is strictly your baby."

"Mother will be so thrilled," he replied. "She's been nagging me for ages to make her a grandmother."

"I wouldn't send her any baby pictures," Keeley said. "It would be too depressing."

Without fanfare, he circled her right wrist with his hand and lifted it. "Close your eyes and spread your fingers."

"Good," he said when she'd done what he told her. "Now relax." He guided her arm toward the sculpture, then slowly lowered her hand until her fingertips struck cold metal and wet paint.

Her eyes sprang open. "Ack!"

She would have drawn her hand away, but Digby held her wrist firmly in place. "It's messy work, sweetheart, but somebody's got to do it, and a baby needs a mother as well as a father."

He was joking—*so why did she suddenly feel like a violin string that had just had a bow drawn across it?* She swallowed. "What do I do?"

Covering her hand with his, he pressed it lightly against the tabletop and began to move in circular motions. "Do you feel it?"

She was feeling too many things at once to know specifically to which of them he was referring. "What?"

"The creative urge. The inspiration. The power to create." He changed the movement of their hands, hopping the pad of her palm across the surface, first in one direction, then the other.

Keeley closed her eyes and sighed, letting her shoulders droop against his chest. "Oh, Digby."

He froze, letting his hand rest heavily over hers, letting the weight of it press her palm against the metal. She felt his chest tense against her shoulders.

She feared he might kiss her.

She feared he wouldn't.

An eternity passed before she heard—felt—him let out a weighty sigh. "You'd better open your eyes so you can see what you're doing," he said, lifting his hand from hers. "I know you're a woman who likes to know exactly what she's going to end up with."

Though his even tone belied the bitterness buried in his words, the double entendre in the remark was obvious. Keeley's heart ached with his pain, with her own. And yet—she had a right to hold out for what she needed.

"I don't know what I'm looking at," she said, focusing on the crushed metal table in front of her.

You've got that right, Digby thought, fighting back frustration, armoring himself against bitterness that could destroy any chance they had together. *You can't see what's right in front of your face.*

"Look at it, Keeley," he said intently. "You said yourself that art has to make a statement. The message is in your fingertips. All you have to do is make it appear. Focus on the colors, the movement in the design, the mood and the message. Only you can determine what you want it to say."

"I want it pretty," she said.

"Then make it pretty," he said. "You can add color or wipe it away, add swirls or make bold statements. Make it soft or make it harsh, but look at it and *see* it and *do* it."

He studied her face as she studied the tabletop, searching for the secrets of her heart as she searched for beauty in the sculpture. After a long moment of contemplation, she prodded a yet-undisturbed spot of pink paint with her forefinger, smeared it into a larger spot and then pushed the pink into a predominantly teal area. She moved her fingers in short, light strokes, blending the paint as she went, before moving to another area to blend the colors there.

After a while, she sat back on her heels to appraise her work. Looking at her hand, she laughed softly. "I feel like I'm back in kindergarten."

Digby turned his hand palm up, showing her his paint-smeared fingertips. "Me, too. I told you this would be fun."

It really *was* fun, Keeley thought, surprised to realize it. With Troy, she'd partied; with Digby, she had fun. *Finger painting.*

"Are you finished?" he asked.

She looked at the tabletop and sighed. "I think so." Then, raising her gaze to Digby's face, she asked, "Is there anything you would do to it?"

There's a lot I'd like to do to you, he thought. *To the tabletop*— He studied it a moment and picked up a rag and offered it to her. "I might wipe off some of the paint in spots, to give it a little more contrast. You know, just a whisper of color over the bronze in some areas will make the others more effective."

"Would you do it?" she asked. "You have a better eye."

"I'd do anything for you, Keeley," he said with a gentle smile. *I would have thought you'd have noticed that by now.*

KEELEY GLANCED at the bedside clock, surprised to see it was just a little past midnight. She must have been sleeping very soundly to feel so groggy after so short a time. She'd gone to bed around eleven, so she'd only been asleep a little more than an hour, but her mouth felt as though she'd been stranded in the desert about a week.

She rolled over and tried to ignore the dryness, but it was useless. Finally, reluctantly, she got out of bed. If she didn't get something to drink, she'd be awake for hours.

The faint glow of lamplight from the living room suggested Digby was still awake. Not wanting to encounter him, she decided to duck into the bathroom and run tap water into a paper cup rather than get bottled water from the refrigerator. A bar of light beneath the closed bathroom door made her pause. As she stood there, frozen, the shower started up with a rattle of aged pipes.

She heaved a sigh of relief. She'd been about to walk in on Digby getting into the shower. Thank goodness she hadn't opened that door!

Intent on getting her water and getting back to her room before Digby got out of the shower, she hurried down the hall. A minute or so later, she reversed her route, carrying the water.

She almost made it.

She should have been at least a bit prepared for the bathroom door to open. Certainly she should have been less surprised to come nose to damp chest with Digby than he was. But they were both stunned, Digby most of all, when she sloshed ice-cold water over his midriff.

He gave a surprised growl and then said, "I thought you were asleep."

"I was," she said. "I just—" She held up the glass. "I woke up thirsty."

An awkward silence followed. Keeley was suddenly aware of how inadequate a satin sleepshirt was—almost as inadequate as the towel wrapped around Digby's waist. "I feel like I'm trapped in an old movie," she said finally.

"Yeah," he agreed bluntly.

Noticing a drop of water clinging to a hair near his left nipple, Keeley reached to blot it away, but Digby grabbed her wrist and guided her hand away. "Trust me, I'm better off with the cold water. If you touch me there, when we're here, like this—"

"Digby."

"Go to bed, Keeley," he said harshly. "Close your door behind you and lock it."

"I don't have to lock my door against you," she said. "You're the most honorable man I've ever known."

He laughed bitterly. "Too bad I don't have a job, isn't it?"

He turned away, leaving her standing there with every nerve ending in her body exposed.

Along with her heart.

13

"YOU LOOK TIRED," Anne said.

"We've been busy all day," Keeley said. "It feels like everyone in Orlando is either planning a Halloween party or getting ready for one. By the way, I ordered an express shipment of Barney and dalmatian costumes. We sold out this morning and people have been asking all afternoon. I thought the mother who got the last Barney suit was going to sob with relief. She'd been all over town looking for one, and she'd almost resigned herself to having to make one."

"Good thinking," Anne said. "How many did you order?"

"A dozen of each," Keeley said. She took her handbag from the desk drawer and stepped aside so Anne could put hers there. "Thanks for coming in on short notice. Who'd have thought our part-timer would come down with the flu on the very day Trish had two root canals?"

"Anyone who's ever been in retail," Anne answered wryly. "Anyway, I'm glad I came. I meant what I said. You look tired. I hope you're not coming down with the flu, too."

"No. I just didn't sleep very well last night."

Anne's eyes narrowed. "Your not sleeping doesn't have anything to do with your—" she cleared her throat with an exaggerated "ahem" "—*houseguest*, would it?"

"Not the way you think!" Keeley said. "It's true that he wore me out yesterday, but not like that." She told Anne about the sculpture-in-progress.

"A metal table and chairs to hang on the wall. Sounds intriguing."

"Don't count on it ever actually getting on the wall," Keeley said. "Digby said he was going to do some more work on it today, but frankly, I still don't see any potential for it."

But when she arrived home, Digby and Chester were in the front yard playing with a tennis ball, and while she knelt to pet the dog, Digby informed her that the *objet d'art* had been hung. He pulled a handkerchief from his pocket and folded it into a long strip. "Your blindfold," he said with obsequious formality, "so you can get the full effect."

Keeley went along, letting Digby blindfold her and looping her arm around his so he could guide her. Inside, he positioned her carefully, capping her shoulders and coaxing her to precisely the perfect place from which to view what he drolly called "the masterpiece."

He lifted his right hand from her shoulder to tilt her head to the perfect angle. It lingered there, warm, gentle and strong, while his thumb traced the bottom edge of her jaw the way a sculptor would refine a line in clay. On the opposite side of her face, his fingertips rested lightly on her cheek and for a moment, only a moment, she tilted closer to them, caressing them with her face.

His nearness was seductive. It would feel so good to slide her arms around his waist and be encircled by his strength, knowing she was safe and protected. But the safety would be an illusion, and a fleeting one. Keeley tensed with the effort of resisting the urge to turn around.

"Take a deep breath and clear your mind," he said.

Keeley drew in a lungful of air and released it slowly as he took his hand from her face to untie the knot at the back of her head.

"Ready?" he asked.

"Yes."

He undid the knot, but continued holding the blindfold in place a few seconds before pulling it up and away with a flamboyant, "*Voila!*"

Keeley stared at the wall, stunned into silence. Yes, it was the old table they'd found at the thrift store. Yes, it was painted the bronze he'd sprayed it, and had been highlighted with the colors she'd picked out to match the upholstery on her love seat. It was the same—but it was different.

Digby had added the other thrift-store items to create a tableau. The parfait glass sat on the table—slanted out, actually, at an angle that created the illusion that it was sitting on the table. He'd fashioned the copper tubing into two soda straws that crisscrossed in the glass, suggesting that two people had shared a soda or sundae. The china rose, with a long stem fashioned from the tubing and smeared with green paint, lay on its side next to the glass. A velvet jeweler's box, empty, its lid flipped open, sat near the rose. And on the very edge of the table was perched a tiny bird of blue glass.

Above the table, the firecracker lamp was mounted with its base flush against the wall, and its tentacles seemed to be spilling moonlight on the table below.

Keeley just stood there, slack-jawed, until Digby prompted, "Well?"

"I'm overwhelmed," she said. "You kept telling me it had potential, but I couldn't see it. But it's so...it's not only beautiful, it's...romantic."

"Tell me the story you see," he said, folding his arms around her.

"A couple has been there, sharing a soda in the moonlight."

He propped his chin on her shoulder. "And?"

Keeley smiled and leaned her cheek against his. "He gave her a rose, and told her that he loved her."

"And what did she say?"

"She told him that she loved him, too, so he took out a ring. He'd been keeping it in his pocket."

"Where is it now?"

"On her finger, of course." She continued studying the sculpture. "Where'd the bird come from? I don't remember it."

"It's the bluebird of happiness," he said. "My grandmother gave it to me when I graduated from high school."

"Your grandmother? Oh, Digby, you have to take it back. I can't let you—"

"I want you to have it," he said. "When she gave it to me, she said I should always remember that happiness grows when you share it."

"Where are the people now?" Keeley asked after a mellow silence.

"Can't you guess?"

Keeley's pulse thundered. "Dancing in the moonlight?"

"They were. For a while."

And now they're making love. He didn't have to say it.
She tilted her head to see his face and discovered him
already looking at her.

"Hold me," she said softly, turning into his embrace.

"I'm a patient man, Keeley—" He released a sigh as
deep as an ocean then, abruptly, he cupped her bottom
with his hands and pulled her sharply against him,
into the unmistakable, undeniable heat of aroused
flesh. "But holding you is torture."

"Then make love to me."

She had not considered the possibility that he would
refuse, but for a heart-stopping interval, when he let
his arms fall to his sides and took a half step back, she
feared he might. But then he brought his hands up to
cradle her face, tilting it, and leaned forward to kiss
her, at first just teasing her lips with his, then claiming
her mouth as he moved his hands down her arms and
around her.

Their lovemaking in Las Vegas had been slow, sweet
and gentle. It was the opposite now. Keeley was not
tentative, and Digby was not patient. They had no
need to discover, only to experience. Technique lost
out to urgency, finesse to raw need, style to expediency
as they discarded clothing and inhibitions.

Keeping one arm around her, Digby haphazardly
tossed cushions from the love seat and unfolded the
bed. Gratefully, groping and clutching, half-dressed,
they tumbled onto the mattress in a tangle.

They joined quickly and moved frantically, their
yearning intense, each touch urgent, each thrust desperate. They moaned with pleasure and growled with
need and cried out with fulfillment as one by one, they
tumbled from ecstasy to oblivion. They lay in each oth-

er's arms, a tangle of male and female limbs, of softness and hardness, of delicacy and physical power while their hearts slowed and their breathing returned to normal.

To Keeley, the silence they shared under the mellow glow of the moonlight lamp above them seemed sacred; to violate it would be a sacrilege. Physically sated, exhausted and exhilarated, she closed her eyes and listened to his heart beat beneath her ear, feeling her own heart beating in tandem with it, while Digby lightly stroked her arm with his huge hand.

Neither of them spoke for a very long time, but finally Digby said, "Universal Studios called today. I'm going to be working there a while."

A while. "But not...permanently?"

"What job is permanent in today's corporate chaos? It'll be full-time for at least a year, maybe more. Possibly up to two."

"So you'll be staying in Orlando...*for a while?*" *A year, maybe up to two. Less time than she'd spent with Troy. God, Digby, don't you realize I don't have enough time to be giving it away in two-year increments?*

"Yes."

"So you can start looking for your own place," she said, willing away the tremor in her voice. "You'll probably want to find something in that area so you won't have to commute." Despite all her resolve, she held her breath, hoping he would hug her tighter and tell her that he had no intention of going anywhere without her, ever. Even knowing that it was a crazy, impossible dream—as crazy as her father becoming a famous movie star and inviting her to Hollywood, or

Troy suddenly changing from a party animal into a family man—she needed to hear it.

You knew this time! she mentally flogged herself. *You knew, and you let it happen. You wanted it to happen.*

"Actually," Digby said, "I looked at a place this afternoon. I'll probably be taking it at the end of the month."

"Oh?"

"You needn't be so shocked," he said. "You made it clear my visit here was strictly temporary. I was just waiting to see where I'd be working before I signed any leases."

"Of course," Keeley said, dying inside. "Well, tell me about it."

He shrugged. "I'm a guy. You know guys don't notice anything except whether the walls are standing."

"You can't expect me to believe that, when I can look up and see what you created out of pure junk." She found his hand and threaded her fingers through his. "We just made love under the moon you hung in the sky."

"What do you want me to say, Keeley? Do I have to spell it out that I'm not enthused over it because I know how much I'm going to miss you?"

"Are you?" she asked, trying not to sound desperate. "Going to miss me?"

"No more than I'd miss a major appendage or two," he said.

THREE DAYS LATER Keeley was in the store, dressed like Alice in Wonderland but feeling like a cross between Scrooge and his overworked assistant. She'd taken one look at Trish's sunken cheeks and watery eyes and sent her home with orders to go to bed.

The part-timer, decked out in a cow suit complete with a plastic udder, was back from her bout with the flu, but she was scheduled to leave at five to take her kids trick-or-treating, so when Michael came in after school, Keeley was going to have to break the news to him that he couldn't leave early to go to the Halloween dance he'd been looking forward to. Ordinarily, she would have muddled through alone, but the shopping complex in which the store was located was having a trick-or-treat sidewalk sale, and she had to have someone watching the table and handing out treats out front.

Oh, yes. She loved her work.

She was in a full squat trying to get the bottom row of Halloween masks in some sort of order when a familiar voice asked, "Do you have any bunny suits in a man's extra tall?"

She stood up and sighed. "No. And you ought to thank your lucky stars for it. If I did, I'd put you in one and put you to work."

"I wouldn't mind working, but I draw the line at a bunny suit," Digby said.

Keeley scowled playfully. "And this from a man who once told me he'd do anything for me."

"Anything but a bunny suit," he said.

"I have a heavy table that needs to go from the storeroom to the sidewalk."

"Just show me the table and tell me where you want it."

"You're hired," she said, already leading him to the storeroom. "What are you doing here, really?"

"I got the key to my new place. I thought maybe you might want to go see it when you get off."

"I'm not getting off," she said, briefly explaining the situation as she shifted stock aside in order to get to the table, which was wedged on its side against the wall.

"I really appreciate your doing this," she said as Digby turned the table upright after carrying it outside and unfolding the legs. "I thought I was going to have to wait until Michael got here to set up, but now I can take advantage of the midafternoon slump before all hell breaks loose."

"Is there anything else I can do?"

She showed him the boxes of clearance merchandise she'd been setting aside for the sale. "If you take these out and use some of your artistic ingenuity to display them on the table, I could finish up the Halloween display before I start pricing."

"Done!" Digby said, picking up the box. Keeley slowed down long enough to flash him a grateful smile before going back into the store.

Michael reported to work a few minutes later and she explained that he couldn't leave early. He took the news stoically, but she could tell he was disappointed.

Digby sensed a problem, commenting, as Keeley used colored dots to tag clearance items for discounting at ten percent increments, "Your Pinocchio looks like he just heard the Blue Fairy was dead."

"He had big plans for tonight, and I'm making him work," Keeley said. "I hated doing it to him." She was too overwrought to resist a hearty frown. "He's such a good kid, and so reliable. So he gets stuck working when everyone else is out playing."

"Could I fill in for him? I know I'm not officially on

the payroll, but I could handle keeping an eye on the table."

"I can't ask you to do that," Keeley said, her heart turning to mush as she looked at his face. He was so sincere.

"You didn't ask, I offered."

"You'd have to wear a costume of some kind. We all do."

"I noticed," Digby said wryly, giving her a lecherous perusal. "Those kneesocks are driving me insane. Do you know how much I'd like to kiss the backs of your knees?"

Keeley frowned in exasperation. "Pervert!"

"I wouldn't mind a costume—as long as it's not—"

"A bunny suit. I know. I just don't know what we have in your size." She called Michael. "Digby says he'll work the table for you, but he has to have a costume. If you come up with something by six, you can leave."

Michael's transformation was dramatic. "Come on back to the Halloween display," he told Digby. "We'll think of something."

A few minutes later, Digby exited the store and told Keeley he was off to the thrift store but would be back as soon as possible.

"The thrift store?" she said.

"I need a pair of boots and a black suit," he said over his shoulder as he walked away.

Keeley's shoulders sagged as she released a weary sigh. *Frankenstein*, of course. It was a no-brainer.

HE DREW CROWDS. Physically, he was perfect for the role, and his drolly sinister grunts and growls as he passed out the treats enchanted the shoppers. Strobes flashed as mothers photographed their little darlings with him.

Keeley could see him through the front window as she manned the cash register, and as she watched him with the children, she relived every gentle moment she'd ever shared with him. He was a giant with a heart to match his giant's body. A loving heart. And suddenly, somehow, nothing else on the résumé of his life seemed to matter.

The crowds thinned out at about eight-thirty, and with Digby's help taking down the table, she was able to close sharply at nine. Digby was maneuvering the table back into the space against the storeroom wall when she took her handbag from the desk.

"Wild night," he commented, the ordinary words rather jarring coming from a tall green monster with a bolt through his neck.

"All Hallow's Eve," she said. "Thank goodness it only comes once a year. Do you want to clean off that makeup before you leave?"

"Not particularly," he said. The sensual note in his tone drew her attention to his face. His teeth flashed white, in bright contrast to the purple-black lips framing them as he smiled. "The truth is, I want to get you alone so I can get you out of those kneesocks and take that big bow out of your hair and kiss you until you don't have a square inch on your body that's not smeared with green makeup."

Keeley wondered how she could remain standing when her knees had turned to rubber. She swallowed. "I guess you'd better follow me home, then."

"I guess," Digby said, imbuing the words with sensual promise.

Minutes later he pulled his truck onto the driveway behind her car. Still remembering his declaration at the store, she didn't quite know what to say to him as they came neck bolt to hair bow on the sidewalk. And the look in his eyes only intensified her perplexity.

"Digby?" she asked warily.

He responded by holding his arms away from his body stiffly, letting his hands dangle limply, and letting out a prolonged, feral growl.

"Digby." The word held a note of warning, but he didn't seem to notice. He just grunted and toddled toward her in a stiff-legged stance.

Knowing it was absurd, Keeley felt panic prickling her scalp. She quickened her step, reaching the door first and getting it unlocked before he staggered the rest of the way. He followed her inside, closed the door behind him and, leering at her, growled again.

Keeley stepped back and said his name again.

Digby responded by grabbing her around the waist and carting her across the room like a sack of potatoes. "Bed," he grunted, pointing at the love seat.

Keeley stood frozen, her mouth gaping open.

"Bed," he repeated, louder.

She pulled out the bed, and stepped back.

"In!" he said, pointing.

She sat down on the edge of the bed and he came over and took the bow from her hair, grunting angrily when the clasp of her barrette proved vexing, and discarding it over his shoulder after finally getting it free.

The absurdity of the situation finally caught up with Keeley as he turned his intense gaze back on her face and issued a sound that could only be categorized as monstrously lecherous. She giggled.

Digby reared to full height and scowled while growling in playful outrage.

Keeley giggled again. Still growling, Digby reached down and scooped her into his arms then laid her down on the bed and stretched out on top of her, pinning her to the sheets. Howling, he rubbed his face all over hers, smearing it with green makeup and then, satisfied with his efforts, moved to her neck.

"Your bolt tickles." Keeley taunted.

With a bellow of feigned outrage, he ripped the plastic bolt from his neck and hurled it away.

"Didn't you say something about the back of my knees?" she asked.

"Ummmmmmm!" he said, and continued ravishing her.

When Frankenstein's monster had finished with dear little Alice, neither of them was inclined to move. Digby chuckled. "You look like you've been swimming in a vat of pistachio pudding."

"That's nothing," Keeley said, pushing up on one elbow so she could see his face as they talked. "These sheets looked like a jungle camouflage canopy net."

"Will it wash out?"

"Probably not."

"How about us?"

"It's the aloe cleansing pads for us," she said.

Digby thought a moment before grinning. "Now *there's* an idea with potential."

"Aren't you ever satisfied?" Keeley teased.

"I am," he said drolly. "But then I look at you and get all hot and bothered again."

Keeley grinned smugly. "In that case—I'll get the pads."

Cleaning up was almost as much fun as getting dirty as they daubed each other with the oily pads and then scrubbed away the oil with Keeley's bath puff and berry-scented shower gel.

Wrapped in a bath blanket with Digby, Keeley rested her head on his chest and wondered aloud how long it would take to get a pizza delivered.

"I've got a better idea," Digby said.

"Is there food involved?"

"There's food. I promise. But you have to have clothes." He gave her bare bottom a playful pat. "Get dressed."

She held out until they were on the interstate before asking where they were going.

"To my place," he said, and then grinned. "I stocked the refrigerator. But it'll take us a while to get there. You can cuddle up and take a nap, if you feel like it."

Keeley cuddled as much as the seat belt allowed and sighed languidly as she rested her head on his shoulder. She closed her eyes, cutting off the world of automobile taillights and three-dimensional billboards advertising thrill rides at the movie studios, but she didn't sleep. She was too exhilarated for sleep, too content to be near the man with whom she'd shared sweet, tumultuous, heart-stopping moments to surrender to the oblivion of sleep. She wanted the conscious awareness of where she was, and with whom. She wanted to savor this contentment, not sleep through it.

In the darkness behind her lowered eyelids, she saw Digby dressed as Frankenstein, so convincing as the mighty monster and so gentle with the children who'd flocked to him, fascinated by his physically imposing persona yet sensing his inherent kindness.

She opened one eye when the truck slowed, curious about where they were leaving the interstate. They were somewhere between Universal Studios and the Disney complex, with the congested tourist area of International Drive off to their left. Digby turned right and told her, "It's not much farther."

Keeley acknowledged the comment with a small sound. A minute or so later, she snuggled her cheek against his arm. "It doesn't matter anymore," she said. "I think it's wonderful that you're a tinkerer."

He didn't quite laugh, but she felt him smile.

As peculiar as it sounded, even to herself, she felt him smile.

The truck slowed, turned and slowed some more. Keeley opened her eyes expecting to see the parking area of an apartment complex, and discovered instead that they were on the driveway of a house which, in her hometown, would have been referred to as a mansion. She sat up straight, stared at the house a moment and then twisted her head to look questioningly at Digby. "I don't understand."

He shrugged sheepishly and reached for the door handle. "I think we need to have a little talk."

I think we need to have a big talk, Keeley thought as he walked around the truck to open her door.

"Where are we?" she asked as they traversed a stone pathway flanked by lush semitropical foliage.

"Windermere," he said.

Keeley had heard of the suburban community, but she'd never been there. She vaguely noted that there were houses similar to the one they were about to enter up and down the street.

The door opened into a tiled foyer, beyond which was a large, open room with a cathedral ceiling. "I'd offer you a seat, but as you can see, there's no furniture yet," Digby said.

Keeley stopped gaping at the imposing structure to gape at Digby. "You rented this place?"

"Technically," he said. "Actually, I moved in on a lease purchase with an option to buy."

"I don't understand." Keeley felt as though she were slowly sinking into shifting sand. "You're not a famous artist, are you?"

Drawing her into his arms, Digby hugged her to him and laughed heartily. "No, Keeley. I'm not an artist. I'm a tinkerer, just as I said I was." His laughter faded as he held her, stroking her back, and a trace of sadness entered his voice. "Keeley, I've never lied to you, but you've taken some things that I said rather literally. And since you seem so intent on condemning me and assigning so many negative qualities to me, I haven't been as diligent in defending myself as I should have been."

"You don't just tinker around, do you?"

"Yes. And no. I'm a troubleshooter, a consultant. Remember that I told you there's always someone who needs something invented?"

"Vaguely," Keeley said, still trying to absorb her shock.

"Well, I look at a problem and figure out how to solve it."

She looked around the room, at the high ceiling, lush

carpeting, polished tile, built-in bookshelves and opulent fireplace. "You must be good at it."

He chuckled again. "Yes. I have a solid track record and an excellent reputation for getting the job done. I also have some solid credentials—a master's degree in mechanical engineering for starters. I even own my own company—D.B. Innovations."

"I've been such a fool," Keeley said sadly.

"I should have explained early on, but my ego got in the way. I wanted you to accept me, no matter what I did for a living."

"I meant what I said in the truck," she said. "It doesn't matter."

"That makes your love all the more special to me," he said. Curling his hands around her upper arms, he guided her just far enough from him to be able to look in her face. "We are talking about love, aren't we?"

"Yes," Keeley said, feeling as though she might burst from the sheer joy of it.

"Thank God," he said, heaving a sigh. Just as she'd sensed his smile earlier, she sensed his joy now, even as he filled with a sudden manic energy. Dropping a kiss on her cheek, he said, "I have a surprise for you. Give me five minutes."

Mystified, Keeley nodded.

"Just—stand here and look at that door. Don't turn around," he said, dropping another kiss on her cheek. "Five minutes."

It was the longest five minutes of her life. She heard him rattling around in what she assumed to be the kitchen, heard cabinets opening and closing, the whir of some small appliance, footsteps, the opening of a door. Then silence, the door again, more footsteps, the door again. And then, finally, the footsteps led to her, and he was behind her, wrapping his arms around her, nibbling her neck.

Wordlessly, he stepped back and reached for her hand, silently invoking her to go with him. Together, they crossed the room and stepped through the back door into a screened wonderland. Water tumbled over rocks to fall into a lighted pool dotted with floating lotus candles. Dozens of paper-bag candelarias twinkled snowflake images to soften the night, and interspersed between the candelarias were huge vases of red roses, dozens and dozens of them, lending their pungent scent to the night air. And in the center of the light and roses sat a white ice-cream-parlor table and chairs similar to the ones from which he'd fashioned the sculpture for her wall. On the table there was a single long-stemmed rose, a milk shake in a tall parfait glass with two straws sticking out, a plate of finger foods and a blue-velvet jeweler's box.

Digby picked up the rose and placed it gently in Keeley's hands. "I'm so glad I could give you your first roses."

Sighing his name was an achievement. Keeley would have thought her chest too full for even the simplest words.

He picked up the jeweler's box and opened it, showing her the emerald cut diamond ring. "This was my grandmother's. She gave it to me to give to the woman I chose to share my life. Will you do me the honor of wearing it? Till death do us part?"

She nodded silently and watched as he slipped the ring on her trembling fingers. "I love you, Keeley Owens."

"I love you, too."

Their gazes locked for a timeless interval before he grinned endearingly. "I know you're hungry, but do you think you could kiss me before we sit down to eat?"

"I think so," Keeley said as she leaped into his arms.

_____Epilogue_____

THEY AGREED from the very beginning that the wedding should be small, traditional and simple—a candlelight ceremony in the country church, in Keeley's hometown. Ivy and roses. A reception in the fellowship hall.

There was a local woman who made wedding cakes, a woman who specialized in punch, and a woman, whom everyone called Aunt Goo, who sang "Oh, Promise Me" or "We've Only Just Begun" at almost every wedding in town.

Despite the simplicity, there was an attendant air of frantic preparation as Keeley, her grandmother and mother conspired over the perfect dress in a degree of secrecy that would have made the Central Intelligence Agency operative appear amateurish. And there were agonizing choices: between three-inch pillars or four-inch pillars. Between raspberry-pineapple punch with fruit cocktail or ginger ale-and-pineapple sherbet punch. Between "Oh, Promise Me" and "We've Only Just Begun."

When the seven-day weather forecast set off a panic by indicating a chance of rain that could conceivably douse the candelarias lining the walkway from the sidewalk to the church steps, Digby jokingly suggested to Keeley that they elope. But Keeley wouldn't even consider it. She'd almost had a spur-of-the-moment chapel wedding in Vegas with the wrong man; now she had the right man, and she wanted the right wedding.

As Digby approached the church and saw the candelarias already glowing in the mellowness of a late—and very clear—afternoon, he understood why. His understanding deepened as, from the back of the church, where he, his brother and the preacher waited for the ceremony to begin, he watched the guests enter the church in their Sunday best, festive as a flock of flamingos. These people who cared about them and loved them—his family, her family, close friends—were here to celebrate his legal and spiritual joining with the woman he loved.

The hand-rung bell in the belfry pealed with the joy of the occasion, and the organ sang out with traditional strains. Virginal young girls in long, frilly dresses lit the pillar candles, as one by one, the overhead lights went out. When the two dozen tall candles staggered on huge candlesticks flanking the altar were lit, Digby and the other men went to the altar, and from there, Digby waited on his bride.

Keeley's friend Connie, so nervous her bouquet quivered, was the first up the center aisle, trailed by the tiny flower girl, Mildred's granddaughter Ashley, scattering silk rose petals from a lace basket. Then the music stopped for a commanding beat of silence, and the fanfare signaled the arrival of the bride.

Digby's heart skipped a beat when he saw her. The high-necked, floor-length dress of lace and satin, so different from the tarty gown she'd been wearing the first time he'd seen her, was perfect. But then, Keeley was perfect. The perfect bride. The perfect woman for him. The only woman he would ever want or need.

In the glow of the candles, she appeared ethereal as an angel. He didn't think she could be any more beautiful, that he could possibly love her any more than he did at that moment.

And then she smiled. Timidly, as any bride should. And Digby smiled back, welcoming her to his side. To his life. Into his heart.

At the appointed moment in the ceremony, he literally and symbolically accepted her hand from Michael, who was puffed up with importance at having been accorded the honor of giving away the bride, and from her seat beside Keeley's grandmother and mother, Anne audibly sniffed back a sob at the beauty of it.

They said the vows, exchanged rings, and were pronounced, in the presence of God, husband and wife. The preacher gave Digby permission to kiss his bride, but Digby hesitated—just long enough to tell her that he loved her before his lips touched hers in their first taste of marriage.

EVER HAD ONE OF THOSE DAYS?

TO DO:

☑ late for a super-important meeting, you discover the cat has eaten your panty hose

☑ while you work through lunch, the rest of the gang goes out and finds a one-hour, once-in-a-lifetime 90% off sale at the most exclusive store in town (Oh, and they also get to meet Brad Pitt who's filming a movie across the street.)

☑ you discover that your intimate phone call with your boyfriend was on company-wide intercom

☑ finally at the end of a long and exasperating day, you escape from it all with an entertaining, humorous and always romantic Love & Laughter book!

ENJOY
LOVE & LAUGHTER™
EVERY DAY!

For a preview, turn the page....

Here's a sneak peek at
Colleen Collins's RIGHT CHEST, WRONG NAME
Available August 1997...

"DARLING, YOU SOUND like a broken cappuccino machine," murmured Charlotte, her voice oozing disapproval.

Russell juggled the receiver while attempting to sit up in bed, but couldn't. If he *sounded* like a wreck over the phone, he could only imagine what he looked like.

"What mischief did you and your friends get into at your bachelor's party last night?" she continued.

She always had a way of saying "your friends" as though they were a pack of degenerate water buffalo. Professors deserved to be several notches higher up on the food chain, he thought. Which he would have said if his tongue wasn't swollen to twice its size.

"You didn't do anything...bad...did you, Russell?"

"Bad." His laugh came out like a bark.

"Bad as in *naughty*."

He heard her piqued tone but knew she'd never admit to such a base emotion as jealousy. Charlotte Maday, the woman he was to wed in a week, came from a family who bled blue. Exhibiting raw emotion was akin to burping in public.

After agreeing to be at her parents' pool party by noon, he untangled himself from the bed sheets and stumbled to the bathroom.

"Pool party," he reminded himself. He'd put on his best front and accommodate Char's request. Make the family rounds, exchange a few pleasantries, play the role she liked best: the erudite, cultured English literature professor. After fulfilling his duties, he'd slink into some lawn chair, preferably one in the shade, and nurse his hangover.

He tossed back a few aspirin and splashed cold water on his face. Grappling for a towel, he squinted into the mirror.

Then he jerked upright and stared at his reflection, blinking back drops of water. "Good Lord. They stuck me in a wind tunnel."

His hair, usually neatly parted and combed, sprang from his head as though he'd been struck by lightning. "Can too many Wild Turkeys do that?" he asked himself as he stared with horror at his reflection.

Something caught his eye in the mirror. Russell's gaze dropped.

"What in the—"

Over his pectoral muscle was a small patch of white. A bandage. Gingerly, he pulled it off.

Underneath, on his skin, was not a wound but a small, neat drawing.

"A red heart?" His voice cracked on the word *heart*. Something—a word?—was scrawled across it.

"Good Lord," he croaked. "I got a tattoo. A heart tattoo with the name Liz on it."

Not Charlotte. Liz!

HARLEQUIN WOMEN KNOW ROMANCE WHEN THEY SEE IT.

And they'll see it on **ROMANCE CLASSICS**, the new 24-hour TV channel devoted to romantic movies and original programs like the special **Harlequin** Showcase of Authors & Stories.

The **Harlequin** Showcase of Authors & Stories introduces you to many of your favorite romance authors in a program developed exclusively for Harlequin readers.

Watch for the **Harlequin** Showcase of Authors & Stories series beginning in the summer of 1997.

If you're not receiving ROMANCE CLASSICS, call your local cable operator or satellite provider and ask for it today!

Escape to the network of your dreams.

Take 4 bestselling love stories FREE

Plus get a FREE surprise gift!

Special Limited-time Offer

Mail to Harlequin Reader Service®

3010 Walden Avenue
P.O. Box 1867
Buffalo, N.Y. 14240-1867

YES! Please send me 4 free Harlequin Temptation® novels and my free surprise gift. Then send me 4 brand-new novels every month, which I will receive before they appear in bookstores. Bill me at the low price of $2.90 each plus 25¢ delivery and applicable sales tax, if any.* That's the complete price and a savings of over 10% off the cover prices—quite a bargain! I understand that accepting the books and gift places me under no obligation ever to buy any books. I can always return a shipment and cancel at any time. Even if I never buy another book from Harlequin, the 4 free books and the surprise gift are mine to keep forever.

142 BPA A3UP

Name	(PLEASE PRINT)	
Address	Apt. No.	
City	State	Zip

This offer is limited to one order per household and not valid to present Harlequin Temptation® subscribers. *Terms and prices are subject to change without notice. Sales tax applicable in N.Y.

Let's Celebrate!

LOVE & LAUGHTER™

invites you to
the party of the season!

Grab your popcorn and be prepared to laugh
as we celebrate with **LOVE & LAUGHTER**.

Harlequin's newest series is going Hollywood!

Let us make you laugh with three months of terrific
books, authors and romance, plus a chance to win a
FREE 15-copy video collection of the best romantic
comedies ever made.

For more details look in the back pages of any
Love & Laughter title, from July to September,
at your favorite retail outlet.

Don't forget the popcorn!

Available wherever
Harlequin books are sold.

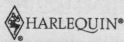

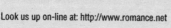

Look us up on-line at: http://www.romance.net

LLCELEB

HE SAID

♥

SHE SAID

Explore the mystery of male/female communication in this extraordinary new book from two of your favorite Harlequin authors.

Jasmine Cresswell and Margaret St. George bring you the exciting story of two romantic adversaries—each from their own point of view!

DEV'S STORY. CATHY'S STORY.
As he sees it. As she sees it.
Both sides of the story!

The heat is definitely on, and these two can't stay out of the kitchen!

Don't miss **HE SAID, SHE SAID.**
Available in July wherever Harlequin books are sold.

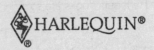

HARLEQUIN®

Free Gift Offer

As Seen on TV!

With a Free Gift proof-of-purchase
from any Harlequin® book, you can receive
a beautiful cubic zirconia pendant.

This stunning marquise-shaped stone is a genuine cubic
zirconia—accented by an 18" gold tone necklace.
(Approximate retail value $19.95)

Send for yours today...
compliments of ◈HARLEQUIN®

To receive your free gift, a cubic zirconia pendant, send us one original proof-of-purchase, photocopies not accepted, from the back of any Harlequin Romance®, Harlequin Presents®, Harlequin Temptation®, Harlequin Superromance®, Harlequin Intrigue®, Harlequin American Romance®, or Harlequin Historicals® title available at your favorite retail outlet, together with the Free Gift Certificate, plus a check or money order for $1.65 U.S./$2.15 CAN. (do not send cash) to cover postage and handling, payable to Harlequin Free Gift Offer. We will send you the specified gift. Allow 6 to 8 weeks for delivery. Offer good until December 31, 1997, or while quantities last. Offer valid in the U.S. and Canada only.

Free Gift Certificate

Name: _____

Address: _____

City: _____ State/Province: _____ Zip/Postal Code: _____

Mail this certificate, one proof-of-purchase and a check or money order for postage and handling to: HARLEQUIN FREE GIFT OFFER 1997. In the U.S.: 3010 Walden Avenue, P.O. Box 9071, Buffalo NY 14269-9057. In Canada: P.O. Box 604, Fort Erie, Ontario L2Z 5X3.

FREE GIFT OFFER   084-KEZ

ONE PROOF-OF-PURCHASE
To collect your fabulous FREE GIFT, a cubic zirconia pendant, you must include this original proof-of-purchase for each gift with the properly completed Free Gift Certificate.

084-KEZR